MILESTONES, MAGIC & MURDER

by Bella Colby

Beresford Publishing House

Dedication

Dedicated to Christine, who introduced me to the real-life Charlie, the supercute Shorkie with a personality bigger than his paws.

Thank you for bringing a little extra magic (and mischief) into the world of Briarvale.

First published in Great Britain in 2025

by Beresford Publishing House,

Unit 34618, PO Box 4336, Manchester, M61 0BW

This edition first published in 2025

A CIP catalogue record for this book is available from the British Library.

ISBN: 978-1-913422-31-8

Cover illustration and design © PlainSight VFX.

Chapter 1

"**H**APPY BIRTHDAY TO YOUUUUU!"
　Oh, no!

The staff of Crème de la Crumb marched through the restaurant bellowing the birthday song like an overenthusiastic flash mob. Leading the charge, the Maître d', his tux starched tighter than my nerves, carried a silver platter topped with a cake so engulfed in flaming pink candles that I expected it might activate the emergency sprinkler system at any moment.

Beside me, Barbara jabbed my arm with a long, manicured, purple talon of a nail. "We had to order an extra-large cake to fit all fifty candles on," she trilled in a voice loud enough for everyone in London to hear.

I forced a smile, praying that the God of the Sprinklers might take pity and save me.

He did not.

I suppose that's what you get for agreeing to a luncheon with the wives of your husband's friends.

The Maître d' gave a visible sigh of relief as he set down the molten, wax-dripping inferno and a heatwave rolled across the table towards me, singeing the edges of a napkin. My face, already well trained in spontaneous menopausal combustion, cranked up a few more degrees.

"Quick, blow the candles out, Josie," giggled Margot. "Before we need to call the fire brigade."

"Noooo, don't," hooted Paula. "I'd like some nice, muscled firemen to liven up this party."

They all laughed, oblivious to the fact that I was one sarcastic comment away from setting the table on fire.

"Josie's going to need a pair of bellows to blow that lot out," Barbara chortled.

The heat from the candles was so intense that the icing was bubbling. I took a deep breath and blew, snuffing out all fifty flames in one go.

Huh! Need a pair of bellows indeed!

The threat of fire over, the waiting staff broke into a polite round of applause before launching into a chorus of 'For She's a Jolly Good Fellow', in case I wasn't embarrassed enough.

"Hope you made a wish, sweetie," cooed Barbara.

Umm. I wish I wasn't wearing a designer cocktail dress in broad daylight with a gaggle of middle-aged women I can barely tolerate. I wish these shoes didn't pinch my toes. I wish my daughter hadn't moved an ocean away. I wish my husband wasn't always preoccupied with work. I wish...

"Time for presents," said Paula in a sing-song voice, dropping a small box onto my lap. I peeled back the leopard print paper to reveal a rhinestone-studded magnifying glass.

"It's for reading menus now that you're ancient, Josie, sweetie," she beamed, as if I hadn't noticed the decline of my ability to read anything without squinting.

I fought the urge to dump my glass of chardonnay over her impeccably highlighted head.

"Open my present next," chimed in Margot. She handed me a gift bag. (Couldn't even be bothered to wrap it, eh, Margot?)

Inside was an explosion of neon pink material.

What on earth...?

I pulled out a tote bag with gold lettering that screamed 'Fifty and Freaking Out' in letters large enough to be read from outer space. The handles were a nauseating lime green, while a smattering of sequins and rhinestones ensured that whoever carried it would leave a trail of unwanted sparkle wherever they went. A wild-eyed cartoon woman clutching her face in horror completed this masterpiece of midlife crisis fashion.

"Isn't it hilarious?" Margot squealed, clearly expecting me to laugh along.

Hilarious. Sure. If by 'hilarious' she meant deeply, soul-crushingly depressing.

Next came Barbara's perfectly tissue-wrapped Wedgwood tea-set. Clearly it had been packaged professionally, because Barbara doesn't do DIY. It must have cost a fortune, but this was a woman who single-handedly kept the diamond industry in business.

"Perfect for our gossip mornings," Paula quipped.

"A toast to the birthday girl." Barbara wobbled unsteadily to her feet, her glass of Château Margaux raised high. "To Josie. To her amazing husband, and another year of living her best life!"

Amazing husband? Best life? Really? They didn't know me at all. But I forced a smile as we clinked our glasses.

"How *is* Gary?" Paula asked. "We haven't seen him in ages." Her tone was light, but I could sense she was digging for gossip.

"Oh, you know Gary, always buried under a mountain of paper-work at the office," I replied, the words rolling off my tongue with practised ease.

Barbara sighed dramatically. "Men! We give up everything for them, and what do we get?" She grinned. "More time to lunch with each other, eh?"

"At least Gary hasn't run off with his secretary," said Paula, whose husband *had* run off with his secretary, last year. "Have you seen the new girl he's hired, Josie? She looks a bit like you did thirty years ago."

Ouch!

The waiter sliced the cake, but I'd lost my appetite, so he wrapped up some slices like I was five, not fifty.

Next followed an hour of chit-chat about exotic vacations, un-grateful kids and new cars. Margot complained about the nightmare of organising an Easter egg hunt for her grandchildren, while Barbara bragged about the Michelin-starred restaurant she'd booked for lunch on Easter Sunday. These women, whom I'd known for years, were the cream of our social circle, but they weren't really *my* friends.

Would they even notice if I left?

I packed the tea-set and magnifying glass into the tote bag and topped it with a couple of slices of cake. Maybe Gary would actually show up later and we could eat them together.

"Not leaving already, are you, Josie?" Barbara called.

"I'm afraid so," I said, forcing a tired smile. "This birthday girl needs a nap." Which wasn't entirely untrue.

We did a flurry of thank-yous and air kisses and I made my escape.

The rain was falling in a soft, steady drizzle as I made my way to my car.

April showers on my birthday. How rude.

I slid onto the cold leather seat of the Range Rover and tossed my presents onto the passenger side. The Fifty and Freaking Out tote slumped against the seat, its wide-eyed cartoon woman staring at me like she understood my pain.

Shivering in my damp dress, I rummaged on the back seat and pulled out my old, oversized, navy cardigan. I'd worn it a few weeks ago while running errands but had shed it in one of my hot flush moments and had never got round to taking it inside. The fabric was bobbling at the elbows, there was a button missing, and it didn't go with my dress at all. Barbara and the others would be appalled at the mismatch. But right now, it was warm, soft and exactly what I needed.

The fuel light flashed as I turned the key. Of course it did. This beast guzzled diesel like a private jet, and parking it gave me panic attacks. But Gary had insisted it was the perfect car to keep me safe, which, between you and me, was Gary-speak for keeping his status intact rather than any actual concern for my well-being.

I sighed thinking of Gary, who had been MIA since this morning.

"There's a band playing at The Kings Head," I'd told him as he'd grabbed a coffee for breakfast. "It's country. They sound good. I thought we could have a meal first, and..."

"Umm... yeah... well, don't book anything," he'd blustered, barely glancing up from his phone. "I'll let you know, eh? I've got work stuff."

Work stuff. Right. Because his property business was more important than my milestone birthday. We used to go dancing, walk along the river... heck, we used to talk to each other.

Not that it mattered. At this point, all I wanted was to go home, kick off my toe-pinching shoes, and sink into a hot bath with an Agatha Christie. At least in her world the clues made sense, justice was served, and the villains got what they deserved.

My house was on a tree-lined street in Richmond, a short walk from the park and the River Thames. A four-storey terrace dripping with original period features and understated opulence. The area was respectable. The kind of place where retired bankers and successful entrepreneurs like Gary lived. Their wives filled their days with private yoga classes, book clubs, and discreet curtain-twitching whenever an unfamiliar car drove past.

We'd lived there for fifteen years, and as the child of an army contractor, it was the longest time I'd lived anywhere.

Today, however, a van with Quicky Locks on the side was parked across my driveway.

I did a double take.

Had I accidentally driven to the wrong house? Had Gary locked himself out? Daft thing. Why hadn't he called me?

Behind Quicky Locks was a removal van towards which two burly men were carrying Gary's antique writing desk.

"What in the name of menopausal madness...?"

Gary knew I hated polishing that desk. Had he bought a new one? That sounded like his twisted idea of a birthday surprise.

I pulled the Range Rover behind a black Ford Transit with ominous, dark-tinted windows.

Quicky Locks man was attacking my door with a power drill. I set off to give him a piece of my mind, but before I got there, another man carrying a clipboard stepped out from behind the removal van.

"Mrs Appleton?" he asked.

He had a face like a weasel. I disliked him immediately.

"Yes. And you are...?"

"Rico Shaw," he said. "Bailiff. I'm going to need your keys."

I guess I wasn't thinking straight when I asked him why?

He nodded, like he'd expected that answer. "We're here on behalf of the court. Repossession order."

Chapter 2

REPOSSESSION ORDER!

Rico said it matter-of-factly, like he was announcing the weather. 'Blustery showers with a strong chance of destroying your life.'

I stared at the clipboard. "Repossession? Of what?"

"Your house," he said, gesturing behind him as if I might've forgotten where I lived. "And its contents."

The words bounced around my skull like a pinball. Repossession? This was my house. My things. My life.

"You have the wrong address," I countered.

Tim's weaselly face twitched, completely unconcerned. "That's what they all say." He wiped the rain off the clipboard, smearing the words slightly, then he turned to the Quicky Locks man, who was zapping the screws into a shiny new lock on my door with a whiny power drill. "How are you getting on?"

"Almost done," said Quicky Locks cheerfully.

"Well, you can hold your horses until I've rung my husband and sorted this out," I huffed.

I pulled out my phone and punched in Gary's number.

"Don't do any more," I warned Quicky Locks.

The locksmith looked at Rico, who nodded for him to take no notice of me.

Charming.

"The number you have called has not been recognised," said a smooth voice on my phone.

I stared at it.

Had the speed dial got itself confused and called the wrong number? Could it do that?

I tried again, cutting the call off at, "The number..."

OK, who else could I call? I knew Gary's accountant. We took him and his wife to dinner every Christmas.

"This is Josie Appleton. I need to speak to Colin Thompson. Now!" I said, trying not to sound like a woman watching her life being packed away like a jumble sale reject.

It took a while before the call clicked through. Long enough for the bailiffs to carry out the large screen TV Gary bought last year. Eventually, Colin answered.

"Josie." He sounded as uncomfortable as a man sitting on a bed of nails.

"Colin, there's been some... some mistake at my house," I told him. "I have bailiffs. They're taking everything, and I can't get hold of Gary."

There was a long pause, and for a moment I thought the line had gone dead, then Colin cleared his throat.

"Look, there's no easy way to say this," he said. "Gary has filed for bankruptcy. And, well... he's left the country."

I blinked. "Left the country? As in, gone on holiday? Oh, he's not run off with his secretary, has he?" I groaned, remembering Paula's earlier comment.

"No, I'm pretty sure Gary hasn't gone anywhere with his secretary," said Colin. "She's already filed as a creditor for unpaid wages."

I felt my knees go weak.

"We're not sure where Gary's gone," Colin went on. "He's... disappeared."

"Disappeared?" I said. "What do you mean, disappeared? Has he joined the magic act in a traveling circus? Decided to become a hermit in the Hebrides?"

"We simply don't know, but my best guess would be Paraguay," Colin admitted. "He filed for bankruptcy independently, leaving you solely responsible for the debts incurred jointly. I'm sorry, Josie."

While Colin droned on in legal jargon about the financial implications, I found myself staring at the bailiffs, still efficiently taking away my life.

Boy, these guys could pack a van.

"We did try to reach you," Colin was saying apologetically. "We sent letters. You didn't respond."

Had Gary hidden the letters before I saw them? How could this be happening? The man I married, the man I thought I knew, had left me in ruins? We'd been together for thirty years. Thirty years! How could he just... leave?

I clicked off the call without saying goodbye.

"Mrs Appleton." Rico handed me a ream of paperwork. "Everything's in there. All in order."

I glanced at the papers. Without my reading glasses, I couldn't make much out, but the words 'collateral against Appleton Prestige Properties' emerged clearly. I knew the business had been struggling, but Gary had told me he'd found a new investment partner and everything was sorted.

The curtains at Number 48 across the road twitched.

Damn it. Nosy Annie was watching. I suppose she could hardly miss the circus on my front path, where a never-ending line of sweaty men were removing furniture from my house like ants at a picnic.

"I'll need your car keys, too," said Rico.

"You can't have my car," I shrieked. Then, remembering Nosy Annie, I leaned towards Tim. "It's *my* car," I hissed.

"Belongs to the bank now," said Rico.

"But my birthday presents?" My voice wavered, despite my best efforts.

"Presents?" asked Rico.

"Yes," I said, my shoulders slumping defeatedly. "It's my fiftieth today."

Rico's expression softened. "OK, well go and get them, sweetheart. It'll save me the trouble of removing them later. And *then* I'll have your keys."

Sweetheart! Huh!

I stomped to my car.

The cartoon woman on the Fifty and Freaking Out bag looked even more horrified as I yanked her off the seat, leaving behind a splatter of glitter. I groaned at the painful irony of the slogan.

It wasn't just Nosy Annie's curtains that were twitching now. Nosy Steve and Nosy Greta were peeping too.

This would give them something to talk about for days.

Quicky Locks man gave the new lock on my front door a rub with his sleeve and handed the keys to Rico, who joined me at the Range Rover.

"Nice motor," he said.

"It needs fuel," I told him, suddenly pleased I hadn't stopped at the petrol station on the way home.

The bailiffs were locking the door, their job done. I'd imagined I'd live in that house forever, but as the door clicked shut, I felt a strange sense of detachment. Just like that, I was a child again, standing in yet another doorway, suitcase in hand, watching another house fade into my memory as my father's job pulled us somewhere new.

Rico handed my car keys to a man with an armful of tattoos, and they all drove away, leaving me standing on the kerb with my crazy tote bag.

"Well," I said to no one in particular, "this is just peachy."

"Everything all right, Josie?"

Nosy Phyllis from next-door was advancing towards me.

This drama would be right up her street.

I took a deep breath, channelling every ounce of British stiff upper lip I could muster. "Fine."

Nosy Phyllis propped herself on the fence. "What happened to your car?" she asked.

"Gone to the garage," I said, which could have been true.

Before she could ask any more questions, a sleek black Mercedes pulled alongside us.

Oh, what now?

The car door swung open with an elegant swoosh and out stepped a man who looked like he spent his days winning cases in the High Court. Crisp suit, polished shoes, and an air of importance that practically radiated off him in waves. In his hand, he clutched a large manila envelope.

"Mrs Josie Appleton?" he enquired.

"The one and only," I admitted.

"My word, you *are* popular today," said Nosy Phyllis.

"It's my birthday," I quipped.

The man held out the envelope like it contained the secrets of the universe... or maybe another bill. "I've been instructed to give you this."

I hesitated. Could I be accepting more trouble? Had this guy come to claim the cocktail dress off my back? But Nosy Phyllis was waiting.

"OK," I said, taking the envelope warily. "Let's see what other surprises I have on my fabulous fiftieth."

Chapter 3

THE ENVELOPE WAS SURPRISINGLY heavy. After the day I'd been having, I half-expected it to burst open to release a swarm of locusts, or grow tiny legs and shimmy across the drive.

"Who instructed you to bring this?" I asked the man.

"My name is Harlow," said the man in a serious tone. "Of Harlow and Fitch, solicitors for your late grandmother, Beatrix Pembroke. Ms Pembroke passed several years ago, but she left very clear instructions. We were to ensure this reached you, in person, on your fiftieth birthday, which I believe is today."

I stared at him, my heart thumping. "My grandmother?" I gasped.

Beatrix Pembroke was a name that never passed my father's lips. My mother's mother. The one I'd always been told was 'crazy and not to be discussed'.

The rain had stopped now, leaving behind dripping gutters and the smell of damp earth. Nosy Phyllis was leaning so far over the fence she was practically part of it.

"Why today?" I asked him. "Why my fiftieth?"

"Those were her instructions," he said simply.

"Open it," squeaked Nosy Phyllis.

I turned the envelope over in my hands. The paper was thick, expensive, and smelled faintly of herbs. It was sealed with an official looking crest imprinted into a splat of red wax.

"Alright, then," I muttered, slipping my finger under the seal. "Let's see what other surprises the universe has for me today."

The wax cracked with a satisfying pop and I tipped out a folded note, a set of keys, and the deeds... to a house... Briarwood Gables.

I stared at the words, my mind a blank. "Is this a joke?" I asked. "Because if it is, I'm not finding it funny."

Mr Harlow shook his head. "I can assure you it's quite real. Briarwood Gables has been in your family for generations. Your grandmother left it to you. The details are all there. It's in Cornwall, the village of Briarvale. I believe it's a substantial property. Quite... unique."

I shivered. The name sounded like something out of a Gothic novel, all eerie creaks and secrets in the attic.

"Josie inherited a house!" squealed Nosy Phyllis to Mr Harlow. "Now that's *my* kind of birthday present." And she hurried away, no doubt to spread this particularly juicy gossip to the other curtain twitchers.

Mr Harlow turned to leave, too.

"Hey!" I called. "What's the catch?"

He paused, looking back, and for a moment I thought he almost smiled. "No catch, Ms Appleton. This is entirely legitimate. If you have any questions, my card is there."

Questions? I didn't know where to start, but Mr Harlow was returning to his car with the speed of a getaway driver leaving a heist.

"Well," I said to Tote Bag Woman. "Now what?"

And then my phone lit up with the faces of my daughter and her twins.

"Happy Birthday, Nana," chorused Juno and Ivy, launching into the second rendition of the birthday song in my honour that day.

"That was lovely, girls," I choked, hastily wiping my eyes, and pasting on a smile.

The twins ran off laughing.

"Have you had a good day, Mum?" asked Kim. "What have you been doing to celebrate? I hope Dad's been pampering you."

Pampering me?

I stared at my beautiful, kind-hearted, happy, unsuspecting daughter on the screen. How could I explain her father had officially qualified as worst husband of the year? No. I wasn't ready for that yet.

"Oh, I went out to lunch with Margot and the others," I said noncommittally. "And you know your father." I forced a laugh. "Always full of surprises. But, hey, I've got some news."

Kim's eyebrows furrowed together. "News?"

I knew that would distract her from Gary's birthday performance.

"Yes," I said. "I've inherited a house. Can you believe it?"

"Whose house?" asked Kim.

"My grandmother, Beatrix. I never met her, but she left me this place called Briarwood Gables," I explained.

Kim's eyes grew round. "That sounds like the setting for a murder mystery."

"Ooh, I hope not," I said honestly. "Because I'm on my way to see it, right now."

I hadn't decided to go until the very moment I said those words. But why not? It wasn't like I had anywhere else to stay.

There was a moment of silence before Kim burst out laughing. "You're going now? On your birthday?" she chortled. "I thought you wanted to go and watch that country band in The King's Head? Isn't Dad taking you to dinner, or dancing, or something?"

Dancing! I couldn't even remember the last time Gary and I went dancing.

"Not tonight, dear. I want to pop down to see Briarwood Gables," I said, hoping to deflect questions about Gary's whereabouts. "It's not every day you inherit a house, right?"

Kim's eyes narrowed. "Where is it?"

"Cornwall," I said matter-of-factly.

"Cornwall? Mum, you don't 'pop down' to Cornwall!" said Kim. "It's miles away."

"I know," I breezed. "But I'm having a birthday adventure. So listen, I really should dash. I have a train to catch."

I didn't actually know whether trains ran to Briarvale when I said that. But surely I could get somewhere close?

Kim made a choking noise, and her eyebrows scrunched together. "You're going on the train? Mum, why aren't you driving?"

"The car's in the garage," I said.

I was beginning to believe that.

"I'll send you some photos from Briarvale when I get there," I assured her.

"O...K...," said Kim.

I knew she suspected something, but I wasn't yet ready to tell her what was really going on.

"Promise me you'll be careful," Kim said. "And call me when you get there."

I smiled at her concern. "I will," I promised. "Give the girls a hug from me. Speak soon. Love you."

The sun found a chink in the April cloud, and I hung up the call with a new sense of purpose. I could just... leave? Like Gary. Start over in some creepy old house in the middle of nowhere? It sounded crazy. It also sounded kind of perfect.

Chapter 4

FIRST, I PUT A search into my phone for Briarvale. I half-expected it to be some fictional place on the Hogwarts line, departing from Platform 9 3/4. Reassuringly, it had a small station not far from Penzance.

"That's a good start," I muttered.

Nosy Steve and Nosy Greta were still at their windows. It was probably the best entertainment they'd had for years. I gave them a cheerful wave. At least I still had my dignity... and the deeds to a mysterious house that probably needed a new roof and an exorcism.

"Time to channel my inner Mary Poppins and fly on the East Wind. Or in this case, the 7:15 from Paddington," I told Tote Bag Woman, tucking the deeds into her safe-keeping.

I had enough time to get there easily if I called a cab. My finger hovered over the call button.

What if my bank account had stopped working?

I had paid for lunch in Crème de la Crumb, but that was hours ago. Maybe I should test my card in an ATM first rather than get into an embarrassing situation over unpaid taxi fares.

I cast one last glance at what used to be my house, then straightened my shoulders. "Right then," I said. "When life gives you lemons, you make lemonade. And when it gives you a spooky old house, you... become the proud owner of a tetanus risk."

I slipped my phone into my pocket, smoothed my dress and gave the nosy parkers across the road a final wave before taking a step forward. And then another. And another.

I was doing this.

It didn't take long before I regretted every life choice that had led to wearing stilettos today. By the time I reached the ATM, my feet felt like they were actively plotting my murder.

Good news: my card still worked.

On an impulse, I withdrew as much cash as the bank allowed... just in case.

I was already halfway to the Tube, so in the interests of saving what little money I had left, I decided against the cab.

I had time... Just.

By the time I reached Paddington, my feet were blistered and raw, but I still had five minutes to spare. That was five minutes to buy a ticket, and find the right platform. OK, so hardly any time.

Paddington was chaos. The kind of chaos that made you wonder how anyone got anywhere on time.

I clip-clopped to a ticket machine like a lame giraffe only for a rail employee to tell me, "Machine's out of order. You'll have to go to the office."

He pointed towards a queue stretching to the other end of the station.

I groaned.

My heels echoed painfully as I scurried to the ticket office.

"A ticket to Briarvale, please," I told the man behind the desk. Then I added, "One way."

He tapped at his computer screen. "You've missed the 7.15," he informed me.

Noooo!

I steadied myself against the ticket window. "When's the next one?"

"Well, the 9.15's been cancelled. The next train's not until tomorrow morning."

I stared at him in horror.

"Hey, don't forget the Night Riviera," called a second ticket officer.

"Oh yeah," my guy said. "The sleeper train. You can buy a cabin ticket..." He glanced at me. "Or just a seat."

Did I look that destitute? I caught my reflection in the ticket office window: hazel eyes wide and auburn hair which looked like I'd been tossed into a tornado and spat out the other side.

But the Night Riviera sounded so romantic, like something out of a 1940s' film noir. It felt perfect for my journey into the unknown.

"I'll take the sleeper," I said.

The price smashed that dream. I zapped my bank card for the cheaper seat, crossing my fingers tightly.

The machine gave a horrified screech, as though my card had offended its delicate circuits. It was loud enough to turn the heads of everyone in the queue.

"I'm sorry," said the ticket officer. "There seems to be a problem with your card. Do you want to try again?"

"Umm, no," I blustered. "I'll pay cash."

"Right. The train leaves Platform 3 at 11.30," said the ticket officer, handing me my ticket.

That left three hours to kill!

"I'd wait in the lounge," he added, eyeing my thin dress.

I nodded. The April night had turned chilly and suddenly I felt it.

The weight of everything that had happened crashed down on me as I sat in the waiting room. Gary's lies. The house. The bailiffs. The mysterious grandmother I'd never met. What if Briarwood Gables was a wreck? What if it was haunted? What if...

I stopped myself. Gary's name left a bitter taste in my mouth. The memory of his smooth, practised lies crept in like a shadow I couldn't shake. How had I not seen it sooner? The way he'd charm his way through meetings, through life. It was the same charm he'd used on me, wasn't it? And look where that had gotten me.

But here's the thing about hitting rock bottom: there's nowhere to go but up. And if Briarwood Gables turned out to be a crumbling ruin haunted by poltergeists and bad plumbing? Well, at least it was mine. Mine to fix, mine to fail at, mine to turn into something new. Now was not the time for thinking about Gary. Now was the time to be strong.

My fingers traced the edge of the mysterious envelope. I'd been too busy dashing for trains to read it earlier. I pulled out Beatrix's letter first, smoothing it flat, and squinting at the neat, flowing handwriting.

Happy Birthday my dearest Josie,

If you're reading this, it means you've reached a rather important milestone... fifty years upon this earth.

First, let me say I'm sorry we never met, sorry that you grew up without knowing me, and sorrier still that you had to learn my name from whispers rather than my own lips. That was not my wish, but life sometimes unfolds in ways we cannot control.

Briarwood Gables is waiting for you, a place of new beginnings. It holds the answers to questions you haven't yet thought to ask. I hope you will care for it as much as I have.

With love always,

Your grandmother, Beatrix Pembroke

The words didn't sound like the ravings of a madwoman.

They didn't reek of delusion or mysticism, as my father had always implied.

In fact, they felt like the warm hug I needed right now. Like they belonged to someone who had loved me, even from a distance.

I let the letter rest on my lap, staring at the ink, willing it to tell me more.

My father had never spoken of Beatrix if he could help it. Whenever I'd asked about my mother's side of the family, my father's answer had always been the same. "Better not to dwell on the past." But I'd learned, in those rare moments when his patience wore thin, that he thought Beatrix was crazy. Dangerous, even.

"She filled your mother's head with nonsense about witchcraft," he'd muttered once, after one too many glasses of whisky. "It's a good thing I got you away from all that."

And that had been the end of it. No explanations. No stories. Just a locked door that I'd been warned never to open.

Would it have been different if my mother had lived?

Would I have spent holidays at Briarwood Gables, playing in its gardens, listening to Beatrix's stories? Would I have grown up with another grandmother instead of a ghost?

My mother's accident changed everything.

In the blink of an eye, I lost not just one parent, but the connection to half of my family. My father had locked that part of the past away, sealing it behind logic and practicality, the way he did with everything he didn't want to face.

And now, here I was. Sitting in a train station, with nothing left to lose, a letter from a woman I'd never met, and the keys to a house I was growing more and more impatient to see.

Suddenly, I felt hungry.

Armed with a plastic cup of something that resembled tea and the cheapest, slightly curling sandwich from the station kiosk, I returned to my bench. After that, I remembered the birthday cake. The cream had squashed out of it, but I ate my slice, and then I ate the piece I'd brought for Gary.

"Nothing for you, Scum-bag Appleton," I muttered with a laugh.

It was dark now. More passengers arrived in the waiting room ready for their adventure. The departure board flickered. The Night Riviera was approaching.

With aching feet and a cocktail dress wildly unsuitable for midnight train rides, I teetered after the other passengers. The carriage was surprisingly warm and cosy. I sank into a comfortable seat by the window and kicked off my shoes. Suddenly, this felt like the right thing to do.

*Who needs a husband, a house, and a bank account," I said to Tote Bag Woman, "when you're on the train to Nowheresville?"

Chapter 5

I DIDN'T THINK SLEEPING in a train seat would be comfortable. Maybe I was just so worn out after the events of the day, or maybe it was the soothing rhythm of the wheels, rocking me toward Briarvale, but somehow, I drifted through the night.

I opened my eyes as the train slowed for a station.

Outside the window, a blaze of gold was spilling hopefully over the horizon and the world was bathed in that magical half-light - not quite night, not quite morning. The sprawling high-rises of London were long behind me, replaced with rolling green hills, and clusters of sleepily grazing sheep. For the first time in forever, I found myself smiling.

A mouth-watering scent of fresh coffee and buttery toast drifted through the carriage from the lounge car. My stomach growled.

"Time for breakfast," I told Tote Bag Woman, who still looked thoroughly freaked out, and left a tell-tale trail of glitter as I pulled her off the seat.

The blisters on my feet voiced their outrage as I hobbled my way to the lounge car and settled myself at a table.

On an impulse, I snapped a picture of the steaming cup of coffee, golden toast and rather promising-looking jam pot on the lounge car table and sent it to Kim. She'd be asleep right now, but when she woke up, she'd see proof that I hadn't been abducted in the night. I didn't want her worrying about me. Then I sipped my coffee as the train sped through the quiet, early morning countryside.

You're not the only one who can flee their life, Gary Appleton.

"Next stop: Briarvale." My heart did a little jig as the tinny voice of the train speaker announced our stop.

"This is us," I told Tote Bag Woman.

I caught a glimpse of myself in the train window as I stood up. My auburn hair was doing its best impression of a bird's nest, and my make-up had migrated south sometime during the night. Perfect first impression for meeting my new neighbours. I hoped they weren't as judgemental as the nosies I'd left behind.

"Let's see if Briarvale is ready for the 'fifty and freaking out' look," I muttered, trying to smooth the creases out of my 'slept in a train seat all night' dress.

But there was no time to waste; the train was stopping. I had to get off.

The morning air was cool and fresh as I stepped onto the platform. Briarvale Station was a neat, red-brick Victorian building with a steep-pitched roof and immaculately painted, white decorative barge boards. The platform led to a path bordered with flawlessly trimmed grass where neat clusters of late-flowering daffodils and tulips danced in a regimental line. The whole place was spotless, but there was an elderly man in a railway uniform brushing the platform... just in case. He was wiry, with a silver moustache so perfectly groomed it could've been painted on, and the creases in his trousers were so crisp I half-expected them to salute themselves.

The train doors hissed shut behind me and the Night Riviera pulled away. As if on cue, somewhere in the distance a clock began chiming. And I don't mean a polite little ding. Oh no. Despite it only being 7.30 in the morning, this was a full-on orchestral performance. There would be no sleeping late in Briarvale.

The man brushing the platform paused, his head tipped towards the sound.

"Do you hear that?" he asked me, blinking behind wire-rimmed glasses. "The Briarvale clock hasn't worked in years, but listen to it."

"Well, it's certainly making up for lost time," I noted.

"Most odd," said the man. Then, his shock at the sudden working of the clock over, he looked at me as if realising he'd never seen me before.

"Percy Henshaw," he said with a polite nod of his cap. "Station master."

"Nice to meet you, Mr Henshaw," I said. "I'm Josie Appleton. I don't suppose you could point me in the direction of Briarwood Gables?"

For a moment, Percy's eyebrows shot up under his cap, then he recovered himself. "Certainly," he said. "Go through the village and take the Polvarren road. It's out the other side of Briarvale, over the bridge. It's probably the best part of two miles." He glanced at my shoes. "But at least it's all downhill."

The blister on my left toe popped in despair.

"So, what are you doing at Briarwood Gables?" Percy asked.

Wow, just come out and say what you're thinking. I'd be calling him Nosy Percy at this rate.

I took a deep breath. "Well, I'm the new owner," I explained.

"The owner!" Percy's moustache twitched with curiosity. "Does that mean you're related to Beatrix?" he asked.

"I'm her grand-daughter." I held out my hand.

Percy shook my hand warmly. "Welcome to Briarvale, Ms Appleton," he said. "I knew Beatrix. Lovely woman."

I felt relieved that he didn't say she was a crazy old bat.

"Thank you." I tightened my grip on my bag. "I'd better see if I can find my house."

The clock struck a last time, its echo fading into the distance as if to say, "Good luck with that."

And then I stepped forward, my heels clicking expectantly against the platform as I wobbled into the unknown.

The road to Briarvale was a single-track, winding ribbon of tarmac, flanked on both sides by hedgerows bursting with spring colour. Overhead, the joyous sound of skylarks performing their morning aerobatics joined the cries of the seagulls drifting inland from the coast.

Idyllic?

Absolutely.

Enjoyable?

By the time I reached the first bend in the road, my feet were staging a full-blown rebellion.

I paused under the shade of an ancient oak tree, leaning against its gnarled trunk for support. "Right, Josie," I muttered, glaring at my shoes as though they'd personally betrayed me. "New life, new rules. No more impractical footwear."

With a sigh, I slipped them off, wincing as my swollen toes met the cool, damp grass. Oddly, it felt... good.

"Remember to watch for nettles," I muttered. And with that, I limped towards Briarvale, shoes in one hand, birthday tote bag in the other, looking like a tipsy teenager arriving home after a crazy night out.

My progress was slower now, but at least I wasn't teetering like a lopsided flamingo. The road wound gently downwards, until I turned a corner and there was the village.

Briarvale.

Cottages with thatched roofs huddled around the immaculately mown village green, their flower boxes overflowing with daffodils and primroses, ivy curling up their white-washed walls. A handsome grey-stone church stood proudly at one end, a tiny school at the other, while the sign on another building declared it to be the 'Library & Community Hall'. Pastel-coloured bunting was strung between the houses and a banner over the road declared that 'The Great Runaway Egg Festival' would take place on Sunday.

I had no idea what a Runaway Egg Festival would involve, but it certainly sounded interesting. The entire scene looked like it had been plucked straight from a chocolate box, and for a moment, I simply stood there, drinking it in.

The village was bustling. A cluster of older school children stood at the bus stop, chatting and jostling each other. Two elderly men lounged on a bench outside Fletcher's Fine Goods; one carried the morning paper, the other a bottle of milk. And in front of the church stood a veritable gaggle of women, deep in discussion. At their centre was a stout woman in her mid-fifties with short, tightly-curled grey hair styled with military precision. She waved a hand theatrically at the church, her voice cutting through the morning air.

"After everything we've done to make those bells chime, they suddenly start ringing," she declared. "This has to be an omen."

I followed her gaze to the church tower, half expecting to see a conspiracy of ravens circling the spire. Fortunately, there was only a couple of pigeons and a blackbird.

The men on the bench bent their heads closer as I limped past. I didn't catch what they were saying, but I got the feeling it was about me.

The women, still deep in conversation about the bells, didn't notice my arrival until I was almost level with them. The ringleader stopped mid-rant as the dog she carried in her arms let out a sharp yap. It was the tiniest, fluffiest dog I'd ever seen, more like a teddy bear than a real animal.

"Quiet, Charlie," she scolded.

With my head held high, I waved my shoes like a flag of surrender, and gave them my most confident smile. "Good morning," I called, picking up my pace as fast as I could manage while navigating the pavement in stockinged feet.

I could feel their eyes following me.

Looked like I'd moved into a whole village of nosy parkers this time.

My plan had been simple: walk straight through Briarvale, find the bridge Percy Henshaw had mentioned, and get to Briarwood Gables. But as I skirted the green, the most mouth-watering aroma of fresh bread and coffee floated through the air, stopping me in my tracks. It was coming from the HoneyPot Tearoom, nestled between a tiny bookshop and a florist. A sign above the door, hand-painted with fat little bumblebees and pink flowers, swung gently in the breeze. Through the window, I could see tables with mismatched china and a counter piled high with croissants and scones. A plump woman in an apron was handing a customer a bacon and egg bap.

My walk from the station in the country air had given me an appetite, and my stomach gave an undignified growl, but I needed to be careful with money if my bank account had been taken for Gary's business debts. The bell over the door tinkled as the man with the bacon bap came out. He held the door open for me with a warm smile, and without any further thought, I went inside.

Chapter 6

T HE WOMAN BEHIND THE counter had a face straight out of a children's story book, with round, rosy cheeks framed by dark curls.

"Hello there, love!" she said, with a smile warm enough to melt butter. "What can I get you?"

I glanced at the handwritten menu on a chalkboard behind the counter. "Bacon bap and a coffee, please."

"Coming right up." She glanced at the shoes dangling from my hand. "Why don't you sit down, dear? I'll bring your order over?"

I nodded gratefully and chose a table by the window. Outside, the church-bell committee were deep in debate with the men from the bench.

Behind the counter, the woman put three rashers of bacon on the griddle, which filled the air with a tempting sizzle. "So, what brings you to Briarvale?" she asked.

"I inherited a house," I told her. "Briarwood Gables."

Her eyes widened. "Oh, my! That's quite the legacy. It's a beautiful old place. Folks around here have been wondering who'd take it on. It's been empty for years." She poured my coffee and brought it over, pulling up a chair and settling herself opposite me. "I'm Sylvia, by the way. Welcome to the village."

"Josie," I said, returning her smile.

Before we could say more, the bell above the door jingled, and another customer breezed in. She was maybe mid-thirties, slim but strong-looking, wearing jeans and sturdy boots.

"Good morning, Sally, love," Sylvia greeted her. "We don't often see you in here at this time in the morning."

Sally nodded. "I've got an appointment with the solicitor in Polvarren later. I dropped the kids in class and settled Benji into playgroup, but it's too early for the solicitor and there's not enough time to go home, so I dropped in for a cuppa," she explained.

Sylvia left me and moved back to the counter. "Your farm sale is going through, then?"

Sally nodded, her loose ponytail bobbing. "The buyer's ready to sign."

"That was so quick," said Sylvia, handing her a mug of tea, and turning my bacon on the grill. "Is it true they're going to turn it into a health spa?"

"They say so," said Sally. "I'll be sad to see it all ripped down."

"Time to start house-hunting, then," said Sylvia.

Sally gave a tired smile. "There's not much for sale in the village," she said. "And I'd hoped to stay close, so the kids didn't have to move school."

My heart went out to them. I knew all about being the new girl, and yes, here I was, the new girl... again.

The doorbell jingled again. This time a tall, elegant woman in a neat navy-blue suit strode in. Her dark red hair was swept into waves that looked like they'd been styled for a Hollywood red-carpet premiere, rather than a village cafe. She clicked across the floor in heels not unlike the ones now abandoned under my table.

"Can I get a cappuccino, Sylvia?" she said, placing a sleek, metal, travel mug on the counter with a gloved hand. "I'm in rather a rush."

I got the feeling this woman might always be in a rush.

"Hello, Madeleine," said Sally. "I'm signing the sale contract this morning. Thanks for your help in rushing it through. I don't know how much longer I could keep the farm going after Martin... well, you know."

Her voice wavered and she swiped at her eyes.

Madeleine turned to Sally with a polished expression of sympathy. "I was happy to help," she said smoothly. "Martin's accident shocked everyone. A great loss to the community. But..." Her face shifted into more business-like enthusiasm. "I have a lead on a property about to come on the market that you might be interested in."

"Madeleine's our local estate agent," Sylvia called to me, pouring coffee into the travel cup. "And this is Josie," she told the others. "She's just arrived. She's moving into Briarwood Gables."

"Briarwood?" Madeleine picked up her cup and turned impeccably made-up eyes to me. "Now that's an interesting property."

"Honestly, I haven't even seen it yet," I admitted.

Sally chuckled. "Oh, you have *literally* just arrived."

Madeleine's lips pursed together, as though she were debating what to say. "Have you met Graham Prescott?"

"No, should I?"

She took a sip of coffee. "He's a land speculator. Very... ambitious. I imagine he'll be knocking on your door soon enough."

I frowned. "And why would he do that?"

"Briarwood Gables is in a prime location. He's had his eye on that property for a long time."

"His firm has bought my smallholding," put in Sally with a sigh.

Great. Just what I needed: a vulture already circling my crumbling nest.

"Well, he'll be disappointed," I said firmly. "Because I have no intention of selling."

Madeleine nodded, her expression thoughtful. "Good. But be careful. Graham's charming when he wants to be, but he's not above playing dirty to get what he wants."

I glanced out of the window, where the committee investigating the wayward bells had moved to the Community Hall. Charming men with questionable motives were not exactly a new experience for me, but the thought of battling one over my grandmother's house gave me an uneasy knot in my stomach.

As if she sensed my thoughts, Sylvia came over with my bap. "There you go, love," she said, placing it on the table with a flourish. "On the house."

"Oh, I couldn't..." I started.

"Course you can," interrupted Sylvia cheerfully. "I'm sure you'll be in here all the time once you've settled."

I swallowed past the lump that had formed in my throat. "Thank you."

Madeleine swept out, neatly sidestepping a man wearing dusty work boots and trousers with various tools hanging from the belt.

"Morning, Terry," said Sylvia. "The usual?"

"I'll take it to go, please, Sylvia. I'm quoting for a job out Trevenna way this morning." Terry pushed a shock of shaggy brown hair out of his eyes with a calloused hand. "Heaven knows the firm needs the work after that lying snake Prescott brought in contractors from London on the Polvarren care home job."

I listened to their conversation as I tucked into my breakfast. Prescott, again? I didn't like the sound of him at all.

"But you're still doing the work on my farm, aren't you, Terry?" Sally asked, her face concerned. "They told me some big developer's turning it into a health spa."

"I hope so. I've already bought in half of the materials for the job," said Terry. "But I don't trust anything to do with Prescott now."

"Maybe you can work with Madeleine on her plan to turn the old tin-mine at Silverbrook into a tourist attraction," suggested Sylvia with a laugh.

"There's no way the council will approve that idea in a month of Sundays," Terry snorted. He took the cup that Sylvia held out to him. "Gotta run. Thanks, Sylvia. See you later."

I finished the last crumb of bacon and fished my shoes out from under the table.

Sylvia frowned. "Are you planning on walking to Briarwood in those?" she asked.

I bit my lip. "Not really dressed for village life, am I?" I sighed.

"I could give you a lift," Sally offered. "I'll be passing that way on my run to Polvarren."

Normally, I wouldn't have accepted the help, but Sally's offer felt like a lifeline. Ten minutes later, I found myself waiting whilst she moved a pair of muddy wellies, a sack of chicken feed, and a suspiciously sticky teddy bear off the passenger seat of her battered Land Rover. The car had a distinct farm smell of damp straw, wet dog and a hint of the half-eaten bag of pear-drop sweets sitting on the dashboard.

Sally jerked the car into gear, and we set off down the lane.

Round a bend, the river came into view.

"I like your bag," said Sally, hurtling towards the narrow stone bridge faster than I would have liked.

"It was a birthday present," I told her, clutching the tote to me as Sally skilfully navigated the obstacle, scattering the family of ducks that were sitting on the parapet.

With a growing sense of anticipation, I scanned the houses we passed. Which one would be Briarwood Gables?

Eventually, Sally stopped outside a long, tree-lined drive.

"Here you go," she said.

I climbed out, thanking her profusely, then turned to face the winding path ahead.

Now to see what my new home was like.

Chapter 7

BRIARWOOD GABLES HAD STOOD empty for over a decade, so I expected it to be surrounded by an overgrown tangle, like the hedge that hid Sleeping Beauty's castle. Instead, the bushes along the drive were neatly trimmed, and a riot of flowers spilled across the freshly mown spring grass. The pathway was too pebbled for me to attempt barefoot, but I hardly noticed my blisters in my excitement and the gravel crunched under my heels in a careful-or-you'll-twist-your-ankle kind of way as I made my way forward.

Finally, I turned a corner, and there it was.

Briarwood Gables looked like it belonged in a fairy-tale. It stood proudly between two oak trees, its honeyed stone walls glowing in the soft morning light. Ivy climbed delicately up one side as though some artist had placed it there, and the slate roof was dotted with tall chimneys. Cute leaded windows glinted in the sun, and the scent of the purple wisteria climbing over a porch carried on the breeze.

Despite its age, the house felt cared for, loved, even in its emptiness.

I caught my breath. I hadn't expected this. I hadn't expected it to feel like home.

Of course, it could be a possible money pit, I warned myself as I headed for the solid front door. But it was also *my* money pit.

My heart soared as the key from Beatrix's solicitor slid into the lock and turned with a satisfying click.

Take that, Gary Appleton.

The entrance hall was grand, with a sweeping staircase you'd see in a historical drama on TV. The place smelled of old wood and lavender polish. Only a faint mustiness gave away its unoccupied status.

There was a tall grandfather clock, its pendulum hanging motionless, cobwebs covering its dusty face. And yet...

I checked my watch.

"That's odd," I murmured. "It's exactly 11.17. The time right now." I gave a laugh. "But even a broken clock is right twice a day, eh?"

Leaving my shoes and bag at the door, I wandered into the living room where the ghostly outlines of chairs and a grand old sofa were covered in white sheets. The mantelpiece above the vast fireplace still bore two brass candlesticks and a row of framed photographs, their glass thick with dust.

Most of them were of a little girl with a chubby face and angelic smile, but one I guessed was my grandmother. She wore a flowing skirt, and her snow-white hair was braided down to her waist. She was sitting in a chair in front of a window, the same chair I could see now covered with a dust sheet. She smiled at a long-haired, grey cat that was curled in her lap, and I tried to picture her there now, smiling at me.

Then my heart stopped.

On the other end of the fireplace a familiar photo caught my eye: my mother on her wedding day. My father had kept the exact same picture on his bedside table. I didn't expect to see it here.

Of course, my mother had grown up in this house. Why hadn't I considered that before? *She* was the little girl with the cheeky smile.

But it was the next frame that truly floored me. Inside was a newspaper clipping: the announcement of my wedding to Gary.

I might not have known my grandmother, but it appeared she had been keeping her eye on me.

I swallowed hard and moved on.

There was a dining room with a long table and chairs with high, wooden backs, and a huge sideboard still lined with dusty china. A music room, where a grand piano stood in front of French doors looking over the lawn.

My mind whirled with possibilities. I could start a bed and breakfast, turn the place into an artists' retreat.

The kitchen looked surprisingly clean.

Had someone been here recently?

A thud from upstairs stopped me in my tracks.

No-one had mentioned the place might be haunted.

A second thud echoed through the house.

"Hello?" I called, my voice wavering slightly. "Is someone there?"

Silence.

I tiptoed back through the empty rooms.

If the house had a ghost, I'd rather meet it head-on than have it sneak up on me. And if it wasn't a ghost...? I armed myself with a candlestick from the mantelpiece.

The stairs creaked, and dust swirled lazily in the coloured light from a stained-glass window mid-way up the stairs. The window showed three women in long skirts. Their solemn eyes seemed to watch me as I crept upwards.

At the top of the stairs was a long corridor with many doors leading off.

There must be ten bedrooms in the place.

Ten!

I half-expected the ghosts of Briarwood Gables' past occupants to come tumbling out to greet me. A tiny sound in the bedroom to my left sent my heart racing.

Gripping the candlestick, I crept towards the noise. An enormous four-poster bed with long, red, velvet drapes stood in the middle of a grand bedroom.

I gulped.

Those drapes made the perfect hiding place. Same as the carved wooden wardrobe and the shadowy dressing screen in the corner.

"Look, if there's anyone here, please don't jump out and scare me," I called. "I've had a bad few days and my nerves are shot."

Nothing.

Heart pounding, I inched closer to the bed.

Suddenly, a blur of dark grey fur shot from beneath the drapes.

I yelped, stumbling backwards, as a Persian cat leaped gracefully off the bed onto the rug. It regarded me with unblinking amber eyes.

"Well, hello there, cat," I said, lowering the candlestick. "Looks like you're the ghost I've been chasing."

The cat meowed indignantly.

I didn't like the idea of stray cats in my house, but this looked well cared for. Moving around so much like I'd done, I'd never had a pet. Timidly, I reached out to stroke it. A warm tingling spread through my fingertips, and for a crazy moment, I could have sworn I heard a voice say, "About time you showed up, witch."

I jerked my hand back.

The cat flicked its tail and stalked off.

I sank down onto the bed.

Ghosts, Josie. Really! It was just a cat.

But then a new thought struck me. It looked oddly like the one curled up on my grandmother's lap in the photo on the mantel.

No! How old did I think the cat was?

Before I could pluck up courage to explore further, a sharp rap on the front door sent me scrambling off the bed.

Visitors? Already?

I opened my front door to find two women standing on my porch. I recognised them immediately from the village bell crisis committee. The stout woman regarded me with an expression that could curdle milk. She held the lead of the tiny dog that had barked at me earlier. No more than ten inches tall, it was the cutest teddy bear of a dog, but by the way it was boldly sniffing around my doorstep, it had the attitude of a beast ten times its size.

Her companion stood half-behind her, as if ready to collapse.

"Umm... hello," I ventured.

The stern-faced woman nodded. "Eva Henshaw," she announced, as though her presence was a great honour. "And this is Florence Bindle. We're the welcoming committee."

I let out a nervous laugh. Somehow 'welcoming' hardly seemed the right word.

Florence offered me a timid smile. "We've brought... umm... well, that is to say we're..." She fidgeted with the bag she carried. "Oh dear."

Next thing, the Persian cat from the bedroom padded onto the porch, tail held high. It came nose to nose with the tiny dog, which immediately lost its mind. It yapped furiously, straining at its lead like it was preparing to take down a lion. The cat watched it bouncing and yelping in frustration, then it turned its back and sauntered off.

"Charlie! Be quiet," Eva scolded, giving the lead a firm tug. "Charlie doesn't like cats," she added, glaring at me as though it was my cat.

Was it my cat? I guess it looked like it might be.

"He's... a very tiny dog," I noted, staring at the pint-sized menace. "I've never seen one so small."

"Charlie's a Shorkie," Eva explained proudly.

She must have seen my blank expression.

"A cross between a Shih Tzu and a Yorkshire Terrier," she clarified.

"Oh," I said, pretending that explained everything.

"Anyway," continued Eva. "We've brought you some essentials. Tea, milk, biscuits." She nudged Florence. "Give her the bag."

Florence pushed the bag towards me hesitantly, her shoulders still twitching from the commotion with the dog.

"That's very kind of you," I gasped.

And I meant it. I should have thought to buy groceries before I left the village. In London, I was so used to a shop round every corner and, as I wasn't the greatest cook, Uber Eats was on my speed dial.

"I'm Josie Appleton," I told the welcoming committee. "I only arrived a few minutes ago, but... would you like to come in? I could move some of the dust sheets."

Eva's eyes lit up like I'd handed her the keys to the kingdom. She swept past me with the tiny dog in tow, her eyes taking in every dusty surface, every cobweb.

This woman made Nosy Phyllis and Nosy Steve from London look positively disinterested.

"My, my," she tutted, running a finger along the top of the hall table. "Beatrix kept everything so nice. Shame."

"Shame," echoed Florence, stepping gingerly over the doorstep.

I bit back a sarcastic remark. After all, they had brought me food. "Well, like I told you, I literally only opened the door a few minutes ago. Obviously, there's plenty to sort out."

"That there is," said Eva.

"It'll be hard work," added Florence, twisting her hands nervously. "Especially at our age."

Our age! I was about to remind her that fifty wasn't exactly one foot in the grave when Eva cut in.

"But that shouldn't bother a *true* descendant of Beatrix Pembroke."

"It shouldn't," echoed Florence with a solemn nod.

Were they implying I was an imposter? Or did they doubt my ability to tackle the task?

"I like your bag," whispered Florence, shuffling past the Fifty and Freaking Out tote, still by the door where I'd left it. "It's very... fun."

However, Eva wrinkled her nose. "Here in Briarvale, we do have standards, you know." And she looked pointedly from the bag to my wrinkled dress and her finger-mark tracing through the layer of dust on the hall table.

An impatient hammering at the door saved me from saying something I'd regret.

"Popular place this morning," I muttered. "Who on earth could be next?"

Chapter 8

A TALL, LEAN MAN in an expensive suit stood on my doorstep.

"Graham Prescott," he announced. He handed me a business card and shouldered past without waiting for an invitation. "I'm here about the house."

Graham Prescott? Wow, I'd been warned he'd call. I hadn't expected it to be so soon.

"Hey," I said. "I don't know what you want but..."

"I'm interested in acquiring this property," cut in Graham. "You're the owner, right?"

"Yes," I told him. "But Briarwood Gables is not for sale."

Across the hall, Eva was practically falling over herself watching the show, while Florence had retreated behind tiny Charlie.

Graham looked me up and down, taking in my slept-in-a-train-seat dress and stockinged feet. "Everyone has a price," he sneered.

I squared my shoulders. How dare he come into my home? I flashed back to Rico Shaw and Quicky Locks guy locking me out.

"Mr Prescott, I'll say this again," I said. "Briarwood Gables is not for sale. Now please get off my property."

Charlie was snarling like a tiny, furious gremlin. I couldn't be sure whether he was angry at Prescott or the Persian cat watching us from the stairs, but whichever it was, Eva's little dog went up in my estimation.

"Come on," wheedled Graham. "This old place needs serious work. More than you can manage."

That did it.

"I am quite capable of managing my property," I fumed.

Graham's face lost its composure. "Listen," he hissed. "I've had my eye on this place for years. I'm not about to let some over-entitled, middle-aged city woman ruin my plans."

Oh, he did not just go there.

I drew myself up to my full height, which admittedly still left me looking at his shoulder. "First," I said, "this is my family home. Second, this middle-aged city woman happens to be the legal owner of Briarwood Gables, and even if I wanted to sell, it wouldn't be to someone who barges in and insults me."

Graham's face turned red. "You're making a big mistake."

"No, Mr Prescott," I said. "*You* are making the mistake. Please know I will stop at nothing to protect what's mine. Now, leave before I call the police."

When Graham didn't move, I pulled out my phone.

"This isn't over," he fumed, backing towards the door.

In triumph, I watched him walking down the drive. And for a moment, I swore I heard a voice say, "Nice put-down, witch."

Shaking my head, I stuffed the business card into my pocket and turned to Eva and Florence. "What a disagreeable man," I said, surprised at how calm I sounded. "How about we see if I own a kettle?"

But Eva grabbed Florence by the elbow and steered her towards the door. "We should let you start your cleaning."

"Oh, really," said Florence disappointedly. "I'd have liked a cup of tea...but yes... we should probably go."

And with that, they were gone, no doubt to spread word of my poor housekeeping and confrontational nature around the village.

I looked into the bag Florence had given me. Inside were bread, jam, scones, biscuits, milk, and tea bags.

"So," I said to myself, "about that cuppa?"

Surprisingly, my kitchen did have a kettle and five minutes later I was sitting at the large, wooden table enjoying tea and scones courtesy of the Briarvale welcoming committee. While I ate, I planned my next move.

I needed food, although the prospect of walking back into town on my heels made my feet want to weep.

I needed to figure out if the ancient boiler in the corner worked before the night turned cold.

But first, I wanted to explore my ten bedrooms.

I climbed the stairs, the floorboards gossiping noisily about my adventure as I went. Each bedroom was furnished with solid-looking wooden furniture. I peeped under the dust sheets to find beds with carved headboards, dressing tables with aged mirrors, and wardrobes with chunky brass handles. Most of the cupboards were empty except for a lining of lavender-smelling pink paper, but in the fourth bedroom, the one with the rose-coloured chintz curtains and the cute porcelain lamp on the bedside table, I hit the jackpot.

Inside the wardrobe was a selection of clothes, perhaps not the height of fashion, but a hundred times more practical than the dress and heels I'd worn for the last two days.

I ran my fingers over soft sweaters in earthy greens, warm browns, and stormy greys. Next to them were pairs of sturdy corduroy trousers and long wool skirts in deep jewel tones, and at the end, I spied a beautifully-tailored tweed jacket with brown suede patches on the elbows.

I grinned, imagining my grandmother striding through the village wearing these. It was exactly what a proper lady of the manor would wear. Time for a wardrobe makeover.

At the bottom of the cupboard were a pair of brown leather walking boots.

"No more tottering around in inappropriate footwear, Josie girl," I grinned.

Was it weird to wear my grandmother's clothes?

Or had they belonged to my mother?

Whatever! They were my best option.

I chose a fluffy blue sweater embroidered with a tiny crescent moon, trousers, and the boots. In the dusty mirror, I barely recognised myself... but in a good way. I'd take the jacket with me.

Was it odd that the clothes fitted me perfectly?

What were the chances I was the same size as my mother or grandmother?

Before I had time to consider this, a cheerful whistle drifted up the stairs.

I froze. Someone was in the house.

Chapter 9

THE TUNE GREW LOUDER.

I peered round the door. Strolling up the stairs was a man about my age. He had unruly brown hair and wore a denim shirt and jeans. He walked straight into my bathroom and shut the door.

I ran through possible explanations.

A ghost?

Nope. Too solid.

A passer-by in desperate need of a toilet?

Did no-one in Briarvale bother to knock?

Burglar? Axe murderer?

Entirely possible.

Damn it! Why had I left my phone on the kitchen table?

Then I heard the unmistakable sound of the shower running.

Burglar with OCD? At least my boiler works!

But while he was occupied, I saw my chance to escape.

I'd get my phone.

I'd call the police.

My heart hammered as I tiptoed to the stairs. However, no sooner had my foot touched the first tread than a sharp bark echoed through the house.

What? Did the house come with a resident cat *and* a dog?

A black and white collie appeared at the bottom of the stairs, a low growl rumbling in its throat.

Yikes!

"Shhh! Nice doggy," I whispered.

Could I throw something to distract it while I ran into the kitchen?

Before I could act on this admittedly sketchy plan, the dog threw its head back and howled. Really loudly!

No!

This time, the bathroom door shot open. Steam billowed out, followed by the man wearing nothing but a towel.

Droplets of water clung to his neatly-trimmed beard and his abs.

Yes, there were definitely abs present... and biceps.

My jaw hit the floor.

The man looked as shocked as I was. He shook the toilet brush, which he wielded in my direction. "Who are you?" he demanded.

I gulped, my brain short-circuiting.

Words, Josie. Use your words.

"I'm... Josie," I stuttered, my cheeks burning in the mother of all hot flushes. "I live here... in this house... Who are you...? In my bathroom... Not dressed?"

"Josie!" The man's eyebrows disappeared underneath his wet, tousled hair. "Beatrix's grand-daughter, Josie?"

I recovered enough to fold my arms. "Yes," I croaked, determinedly trying *not* to look at his chest.

Focus on those melting chocolate eyes.

Oh, they're still distracting.

"Wow, it's been a long time waiting for you to show up," the man said. "I was beginning to think you weren't real."

Wait! What?

I sniffed. "Oh, I assure you, I'm very real. And you are...?"

"Tom." He held out a dripping hand and then changed his mind. "Tom Carver. Umm, I'm the caretaker." He gestured to his current state of undress. "I... umm... wasn't expecting you."

"I can see that," I snarked. "And does 'caretaking' involve bathing in my bathroom?"

Tom grinned sheepishly. "My caravan doesn't have a shower," he explained. "But don't worry. Now I know you're here, I'll swim in the river instead."

The river! Was he serious?

At the bottom of the stairs, the dog gave another bark.

"Hey, quiet, Murphy," Tom called.

The dog's tail wagged furiously.

Tom gave me a reassuring nod. "Don't worry, he's friendly."

I eyed Murphy dubiously. I wasn't used to dogs any more than I was used to cats.

Tom's eyes twinkled. "I should probably put some clothes on. Don't want a scandal with the new lady of the manor."

"Good idea," I squeaked.

As Tom disappeared back into the bathroom, I turned back to the dog who tilted his head quizzically.

"Hey, don't judge me," I muttered. "You try keeping your cool when Mr Rugged-and-Handsome pops out of nowhere wearing nothing but a towel."

I started to inch my way down the stairs, but I didn't have the nerve to get to the bottom with the dog standing guard. Thankfully, Tom reappeared a few minutes later, now clothed in clean jeans and a check shirt.

"So," he said, clapping his hands together, "that's the awkward introductions out of the way. What do you want to know? I guess no-one told you I lived here?"

"You *live* here?" I gasped.

A flat-mate wasn't what I thought I'd signed up for.

"Well, in the caravan out the back," Tom explained.

Huh! Only a slight improvement.

Tom must have sensed my unease because his expression softened. "I know it's a bit unconventional, but I've been caretaker here for years. Beatrix let me stay in the van when I ran into... some hard times," he explained. "In return, I kept the place in shape."

"You haven't done much dusting," I quipped.

Tom laughed. "No, but I've done everything else. Briarwood Gables is more than just a job. It's my home."

His passion for the place caught me off guard.

"I understand," I said, surprising myself with the sincerity in my voice.

Tom's face lit up with relief, but before he could say anything else, his phone rang.

"A burst pipe?" he said to the caller. "Yeah, sure I can take a look." He ended the call with a quick tap. "Sorry, there's a plumbing emergency over in Trevenna. I'm the local handyman as well as your caretaker." He hesitated. "But... umm... maybe I can show you round the gardens, when I've finished?"

"OK," I said, before I'd thought about it.

"Great," Tom grinned. "Come on, Murphy."

Tom hurried off, Murphy trotting at his heels.

Well, that was an unexpected twist.

But I still needed food.

As I headed towards the front door, the grandfather clock caught my eye. The hands pointed to 3.23, yet the pendulum wasn't moving.

Hadn't they been saying 11.17 earlier?

Curious, I stepped closer.

Maybe I could fix it.

I turned the key in the door, admiring the intricate marquetry along the case.

"I'll have you ticking in no time," I told it, reaching for the clock hand.

Suddenly, the air around me crackled.

The cat was racing down the stairs like the hounds of hell were on its tail.

"Stop!" screeched a voice.

But it was too late: my fingers had already closed around the hour hand.

And then, the world exploded.

A blast of raw energy knocked me off my feet. I sailed through the air, catching a glimpse of the cat's horrified face as I hurtled across the hallway before hitting the wall on the other side of the room. I bounced off, crashing into the hall table with my head.

And then everything went black.

A pounding on the front door brought me back.

"Josie! Are you there?"

Struggling to sit up, I came face to face with the cat.

"Oh, good, you're not dead," said a voice.

I looked round to see who was speaking. There was no-one, but my head ached something fierce.

Groaning, I dragged myself off the floor, wiping a trail of blood that ran from a gash on my forehead.

The air still buzzed with a strange energy as I stumbled to the door and fumbled with the lock.

Tom stood on the step, Murphy at his heel.

"Tom?" I muttered." What...?"

He looked at me, his face pale. "There's a body by the greenhouse."

Chapter 10

I STARED AT TOM. I must have misheard him.

"I'm sorry, did you say a body?" I stuttered. "As in, a dead body?"

Tom nodded grimly. "As dead as they come, I'm afraid. I've already rung the police." He peered at my forehead. "Are you OK? You've got blood running..."

I winced as I touched my head. "Yeah, I hit it on the table after I got a shock..." I stopped.

How on earth did I get an electric shock from a wind-up grandfather clock?

"A shock?" Tom asked, offering me a handkerchief.

"Umm... yes," I blustered, dabbing at the blood. "Not an electric shock... because that would be stupid, right? No, just... a noise startled me... I must have passed out." I realised I was rambling and shut up.

"Passed out!" Tom peered at me, a mixture of alarm and concern. "That's a nasty bump you have. Looks like you've gone ten rounds. You sure you're all right?"

"I'm fine," I cut in. "But what about this body?"

Tom nodded. Without another word, we walked round the house to a side gate in a crumbling brick wall. Looking for a body wasn't exactly how I imagined my first stroll through my garden.

Behind the wall was a freshly dug vegetable patch, where neat rows of tiny green shoots were beginning to sprout.

"Wow, did you do all this?" I asked Tom.

"Yeah," he said. "I've got early potatoes and some carrots, and the tomatoes and peppers will be ready for planting out soon."

We turned a corner and the greenhouse came into view. And there, sprawled across the path, was a man.

I recognised him immediately. "It's Graham Prescott!" I gasped.

"That's right." Tom sounded surprised. "You know him?"

"He called here earlier, wanting to buy the house," I explained. "I sent him packing."

The implication of this suddenly hit me. The man I'd argued with that morning was now dead in my garden!

"I don't suppose this is some sort of 'welcome to the neighbourhood' prank?" I quipped shakily.

Tom shook his head.

Then my gaze fell on a familiar object near Prescott's outstretched hand. A candlestick. And I was sure it was exactly the same as the one I'd taken from the mantelpiece earlier.

My candlestick! My fingerprints!

My stomach lurched. This couldn't be happening.

The distant wail of sirens jarred with the gentle cooing of a pigeon on the greenhouse roof. I didn't know whether to be relieved, or grab the candlestick and run.

But it was too late for running.

An ambulance pulled onto the drive, followed by a police car, its lights flashing. It was joined by a sleek unmarked car. As the first officer stepped out of his car, notepad in hand, I couldn't help but wonder who was the real killer? And more importantly, would anyone believe it wasn't me?

Murphy greeted the paramedics with an enthusiastic, wagging tail, and Tom pointed them in the direction of Graham Prescott, but before he went, one of the ambulance crew looked at me.

"That's a nasty gash on your head," he noted.

"I'm perfectly fine," I started.

"She thinks she passed out," put in Tom.

I glowered at him.

"You could have a concussion," said the paramedic. "I'll take a look in a moment."

I put my hand up. He was right: there was a bump the size of an egg on my forehead. But covering it with my hand eased the pain, even though it made my fingers tingly. I hoped the tingling wasn't a side effect of concussion.

The man from the unmarked car strode over with purposeful efficiency. "DI Brett Holloway," he announced. "What happened here? Who found the body?"

"I did," said Tom. "Tom Carver. I spotted him when I went to water the tomatoes."

DI Holloway turned to me, his sharp brown eyes taking in my injury. "Were you with Mr Carver?"

"No, I was inside the house," I explained.

"And you are...?"

"Josie Appleton, owner of Briarwood Gables."

It felt good to say that.

The DI looked momentarily surprised. "I thought this place was unoccupied," he said. "Has been all the time I've been in Briarvale."

I sniffed. "Not anymore," I told him.

He gave me an unimpressed nod. "What happened to your head?"

My mind raced. How on earth was I supposed to explain what happened without sounding completely bonkers? 'Sorry officer, but the grandfather clock tried to kill me' didn't seem like a rational defence.

"I tripped and collided with the hall table," I told him, trying to cover the gash with my still-tingling hand. "I wasn't fighting with Mr Prescott, if that's what you think."

The DI's sharp eyes bored into me. He didn't believe me. I could tell.

"Right, how about you both step inside and Officer Chen will take your preliminary statements," he said.

Behind us, an officer was stringing blue-and-white police tape around the scene while another snapped photos of the body and greenhouse from every angle. The paramedics, having done all they could for Graham Prescott, were now fussing over Murphy and admiring Tom's vegetable patch.

Officer Chen was a friendly, easy-going man with a warm smile. It was the kind of smile that made you want to spill your deepest secrets before you even realised you were talking, which was probably why he was the one taking statements.

"You folks just moved in?" he asked, noting the dust sheets as he followed me through to the kitchen.

"I live in the caravan out back," Tom told him.

"But *I* only arrived this morning," I added, in case Officer Chen thought that we were a couple.

"Bad luck to have a murder in your garden already," said Officer Chen.

Was he now insinuating I had something to do with that? And I thought about the candlestick. How had it got outside?

"I'll put the kettle on," I said.

Thank goodness the welcome committee had brought some tea.

"Great idea," said Officer Chen, settling himself at the kitchen table with his notebook. He turned to Tom. "Tell me what happened?"

Tom sat down with a sigh. "I'd been out on a job and..."

"Job? Where?" Chan cut in.

"A plumbing callout over in Trevenna," said Tom.

Chen's pen hovered over the paper. "Name? Address?" he asked.

"It was a Mr Smith. Brook Cottage." Tom shifted in his chair. "But it won't be much of an alibi. There was no-one there."

"So, you did the job while this 'Mr Smith' was out?" said Chen.

I didn't like the way he said 'Mr Smith'.

Tom took a deep breath. "That's the funny thing," he said. "I got a call from this guy. He said his name was Smith: said he had a plumbing emergency."

"What time was this?" said Chen, tapping his pen on the table.

"Right after I met Josie." Tom looked at me. "About two o'clock."

I nodded, checking the cupboards to see if I possessed more cups. Happily, there was a whole cupboard full.

"But when I got to the cottage, the place was empty," Tom went on. "The neighbour told me the owner, Mrs Pendle, died a couple of months ago and her family was selling. So, I drove back to Briarwood Gables. That's when I found Graham Prescott."

I poured the tea and set the cups on the table. If Officer Chen thought Tom had a weak alibi, he didn't show it. Instead, he turned to me with an encouraging smile.

"What's your side of the story?"

"I was in the house all the time."

"And you didn't hear any scuffles outside?"

"No."

"And your head?"

"I fell. But I'm feeling much better now."

That wasn't a lie. Running my hand over my forehead, the bump had gone down considerably, and the bleeding had stopped.

Officer Chen pushed his chair back. "So, why was Graham Prescott in your garden, Mrs Appleton?"

"I... I have no idea," I stuttered.

"Well, that should be all for now," said Officer Chen, but before we could move, DI Holloway strode into the kitchen.

"Mrs Appleton," he said. "We have two witnesses who claim to have seen an altercation between yourself and the deceased this morning. I think you need to explain what that was about?"

Chapter 11

I CAUGHT MY BREATH.

Argument?

Witnesses?

That could only mean Eva and Florence. Some welcome committee!

I gulped. "Umm, nothing happened really," I started. "Mr Prescott wanted to buy Briarwood Gables. I told him it wasn't for sale. He argued a bit... and then he left."

DI Holloway was staring at me with unforgiving eyes. "So, you didn't say, 'I will stop at nothing to protect what's mine'?"

His words hung heavy in the air.

My mouth went dry. "I... I..." I swallowed hard. "I might have said something along those lines. But I didn't mean I was going to slog him over the head with a candlestick. I just didn't want to sell, and he was being pushy and, quite honestly, threatening."

"So, you know Mr Prescott was bludgeoned with a candlestick?" said Holloway.

I frowned at him. "Of course I do," I snapped. "It was right there on the path, covered in blood. Anyone could have figured out what happened to him."

I stopped. Getting annoyed with a detective who was almost accusing you of murder was probably not a smart move.

Through the open door into the hallway, I heard Eva's commanding voice.

"Oh, it was quite the spectacle, officer! Graham stormed out, red-faced and spluttering. I've never seen him so upset!"

"He *was* upset," wavered Florence. "Spluttering upset."

I clenched my teeth. Unbelievable!

"Yes, he was upset," I said resolutely. "And yes, he was spluttering. But he was very much alive when he left my door, and I didn't see him again until Tom told me he was dead on the path."

"Mrs Appleton, why was Mr Prescott in your garden?" Officer Chen asked again.

"I already explained, I don't know," I protested. "I told him to leave. He had no business being there. I don't know why he was by the greenhouse. He must have gone snooping round for something."

Chen's pen flew across the notebook, while the DI looked at me for a long moment.

Finally, he nodded. "Thank you, Mrs Appleton," he said. "I'm afraid we will be conducting our investigation for some time. We'll try to keep the interruptions to a minimum."

The police left, leaving me sitting at the table with Tom.

I slumped into my chair, wrapping my hands around my tea. Across the table, Tom sat stiffly, his arms folded.

I couldn't help wondering, could he have done this? He had access to the grounds and knew the layout. But why? Did he think that I might sell to Graham, and he would lose his home here? It seemed an extreme measure, but Tom had made a point of telling me how much this place meant to him. He seemed nice enough, but then Gary hadn't seemed the type to abandon his wife for Paraguay to avoid his financial problems.

Tom huffed a breath, rubbing a hand over his face. "They think one of us did it."

I glanced at him, my fingers tightening around the cup. "Yeah," I admitted. "They do."

Tom had found the body. He had no alibi. Was he the killer?

"That phone call, the phoney job, it was a set-up to get me out of the way," he sighed.

"That would mean someone planned to kill Graham Prescott," I gasped.

Tom leaned forward, resting his elbows on the table. "*You* argued with him this morning," he said carefully.

I winced. "And I was there when you got the call about the job," I countered. "It wasn't me who set you up."

"And you didn't see Graham after I left?" Tom asked.

"I *told* you, I didn't have any food, so I was going into town to buy some, and... well... I got knocked out," I objected, rubbing my still-tender head. "I did *not* fight with Mr Prescott, and I certainly didn't kill him."

Tom took a thoughtful sip of his tea. "You don't have any food?"

"Well, Eva and Florence brought me biscuits and stuff just in time to watch me argue with the soon-to-be-dead guy. That's all I've got," I admitted.

"So, you've been knocked unconscious and had an entire murder investigation on no lunch?" Tom chuckled.

"Exactly." Then I frowned. "Speaking of Eva and Florence, can you believe they'd heard about the murder and turned up to blab to the police? If we're talking about being set up, how about *that*?"

Tom shook his head. "When you know Eva Henshaw, you'll understand she makes it her business to monitor everything that happens in Briarvale." He pushed back his chair. "Come on, then."

"Pardon?"

"Come on."

"Where are we going?"

"My caravan. I'll make something to eat," he said, already heading for the door. "And I'll show you around the garden."

I hesitated. Should I really be going anywhere alone with someone I half-suspected of murder? But I was hungry. Even if Tom only made beans on toast, it would be better than Eva and Florence's offerings, which I might just throw in the bin after their betrayal.

"Come on," said Tom from the doorway. "I promise to keep my clothes on."

I laughed, even though my face had given way to a hot flush that had nothing to do with my wayward hormones.

"Well, when you put it like that, how can I refuse?"

Chapter 12

M URPHY WAS PLAYING WITH the ambulance crew when we stepped outside. The paramedic gave him a final scratch behind the ears before walking over to me.

"Let's have another look at that head of yours," he said.

I sat on a wooden bench at the side of the vegetable patch while he gently patted my forehead. "Not as bad as I first thought," he admitted. "Keep an eye out for dizziness or nausea, but I think you'll live."

"That's a relief," I said.

Murphy gave a sharp bark, as if agreeing, before bounding after a butterfly.

Tom nodded toward the trees at the edge of the garden. "Come on, let's get out of this chaos."

I followed him, ducking under a low branch as we wove our way through to a small, wooded area. The ground was dappled with the sunlight filtering through the leaves. The sound of running water grew louder, and as we emerged from the wood, I found myself beside a cheerful little river. Nestled on the edge of the trees was a vintage caravan, slightly battered but clearly well cared for.

"That's where you live?" I asked, unable to keep the surprise from my voice.

"Home sweet home," Tom said, patting the exterior affectionately. "She might not look like much, but she's got it where it counts."

To one side of the van was a well-stocked woodshed, and two hens pecked contentedly at the ground. Murphy immediately went into sheep dog mode, running round them and herding them towards us.

"Josie, meet Hetty and Betty," Tom said, gesturing at the hens. "I got them when they closed the big chicken farm on the other side of Polvarren."

"Oh." I eyed the hens warily. "It's nice you have fresh eggs."

The hens clucked their annoyance at Murphy's herding, but luckily for them, the dog got distracted by the jangle of a bell. Next minute, a sheep trotted toward us, tail flicking like an overgrown, woolly dog.

"And this troublemaker," Tom said with a grin, "is Houdini. He's got a knack for escaping any enclosure I put him in, so I don't bother now. I bought the bell so I can always find him."

I watched apprehensively as Houdini walked over to Tom, who scrubbed the rough, shaggy head. "A sheep? Named Houdini? Of course, why not?"

"Oh, that's only the start of the menagerie," said Tom, his eyes twinkling. "There are my ducks, Bonnie and Clyde. They're on the river most of the day, but they come back later on for some feed. Then there's Agatha." He pointed through the trees to where a goose was strutting on the riverbank. "She can be a bit moody, and she's rather obsessed with shiny objects, so if you lose any spoons, keys, buttons, jewellery or your phone, you'll know who to blame."

"My phone!" I gasped.

Tom laughed. "She's only stolen mine once," he told me. "But she dropped it in a puddle when I tried to take it off her, so I needed a new one anyway."

"Umm, I'll stay clear of Agatha," I shuddered.

Tom chuckled. "And you probably should be wary of Mr Tuppyhead, too."

"Who?"

"The goat. One of Sally Barnes' kids named him Mr Tuppyhead. I thought it was cute."

"It is," I agreed.

"Anyway, he's mostly fine, but he does get a bit territorial. If he starts eyeing you up, back away slowly."

My alarm must have shown because Tom laughed. "Don't worry, you'll get used to it," he assured me. "Right, let's get some food."

Keeping my eye on the chickens, I picked my way to Tom's caravan. The space was small but cosy with wooden shelves filled with books and a few plants, and a sturdy old stove in the corner.

"Make yourself at home," Tom said, picking up a pan.

I perched on the built-in bench as Tom set to work, moving with the confidence of someone who knew his way around a cookery book. He didn't look like the sinister murderer I'd considered earlier.

"I was expecting beans on toast," I admitted.

Tom stopped midway through chopping an onion and raised an eyebrow. "I'm offended."

Murphy trotted over and flopped down at my feet.

"He likes you," said Tom, throwing some herbs into the pan.

As he chopped and stirred, he told me the story of how Murphy got his name.

"So," I said, trying not to laugh. "A sheepdog puppy barrels in, makes you drop a flowerpot on the only rock in sight, and you immediately decide he's a living example of Murphy's Law?"

"The flowerpot smashed on the one rock for yards around. What were the chances? So, Murphy seemed fitting. If there's a chance something can happen, then it will," Tom explained.

Tom chatted amiably about the animals and the house while he cooked, and by the time he set a plate in front of me, I was almost drooling at the smell. The meal, some sort of spicy vegetable stew with thick slices of homemade bread, was the best thing I'd ever tasted.

"It's Spiced Vegetable Chowder," he said. "Your grandmother made if for me when I first arrived."

"Really? Well, it's way better than beans on toast," I admitted between mouthfuls. "It's even better than the food they serve at Crème de la Crumb. And it's definitely better than anything I'd cook."

"I could show you the recipe," said Tom. "Beatrix would have liked that. But I'm sure you're being modest."

"No," I insisted. "Did you know you can turn pasta into cement if you boil it long enough? When I'm cooking, it *will* be beans on toast."

There was a silence. I don't know why I'd said that. It wasn't like I was going to cook for the man. Hell, I was married.

The thought of Gary soured the taste in my mouth. Truth was, I'd felt alone for a long time. How could he just leave me in such a mess? For a moment, tears stung my eyes.

"Is everything OK?" Tom asked.

"Onions. They make your eyes run." I sniffed. I pulled a handkerchief out of my pocket to wipe the tear that had escaped and spilled down my cheek, and Graham Prescott's business card fell onto the table. I ripped it in half and tossed it into the bin at the side of the cooker. "I don't need that anymore," I said. "But I'd like you to show me how to cook my grandmother's stew someday."

After we finished eating, Tom took me on a tour around the grounds. The river meandered lazily beside us, the orchard just beyond with the rows of trees budding with new leaves, full of promise for the coming months.

As we walked, Tom pointed out a fountain shaped like a giant teacup, and a row of bushes that I could only describe as drunken animals.

"Is that... a giraffe doing the can-can?" I asked, squinting at a particularly lopsided shrub.

"Ah, that's Gerald," Tom said fondly. "He's had a few too many beers, bless him. I've tried to straighten him out, but he always leans back to the left. Must be the way the wind blows."

By the time we made it back to Briarwood Gables, the police presence had thinned. The crime scene tape was still up, but Graham's body was gone.

I exhaled slowly. "That's a relief."

Tom glanced at me. "You going to be alright in there by yourself?"

I hesitated, then nodded. "Yes. Thanks," I added.

At that moment, my phone rang and Kim's face flashed onto the screen.

Tom gave me a small nod. "I'll leave you to it, then. Good to finally meet you, Josie."

"Thanks for the meal," I called as I stepped away to answer the call.

Chapter 13

"**H**ey, Mum. I got the photo of your breakfast on the train," smiled Kim. "Looks like fun. How's the house?"

"It's great," I said without hesitation. "A bit dusty, but you should see the garden. Juno and Ivy will love it. And there are ten bedrooms, so I've got lots of room next time you're over from Boston."

"You mean, you're staying there?" Kim's eyes opened wide.

I frowned. "Of course. Why not?"

"I assumed you'd sell it, that's all," said Kim. "I mean, what about Dad's job? He needs to stay in London, doesn't he?"

"Umm, I don't know about that," I blustered.

"Well, I've never heard him talk about moving out of the city," said Kim.

"Me neither," I muttered, "but then I'm not in the loop much these days."

Kim was peering at the phone screen. "Mum, have you got a cut on your head?" she asked.

"Oh, I bumped it on the table in the hallway," I told her. "The ambulance guy said it was nothing."

"You had to call an ambulance?" squeaked Kim.

"Well, not for this little bump," I blustered. "There just happened to be a paramedic around." I glanced over at the crime scene tape by the greenhouse. "It's been... an eventful day."

I wasn't about to tell her how eventful.

"Is Dad there with you?" Kim asked. "Because I tried to call him earlier and I couldn't get through."

"The signal's a bit spotty," I told her. "And I need to sort out Wi-Fi. Look, love, my phone's running out of battery, so I'll have to go. But don't worry, I'm fine. I'll call you tomorrow. Kisses to Juno and Ivy."

I sighed as I hung up. Tomorrow I'd tell Kim the truth, I promised myself. After I'd had a good night's sleep and got things straight in my head.

"Right," I muttered as I headed for the kitchen. "A cup of tea and then I'm going to bed before something else happens, like a meteor falls on the lawn, or a tap-dancing squirrel comes out of the pantry?"

"I'd pay to see that," said a smooth voice.

I whirled around, "Who...? Who said that?" I demanded, my eyes darting around the empty kitchen.

"Over here, genius," the voice drawled.

My gaze landed on the large, grey cat lounging on the windowsill. Its whiskers quivered like it was laughing at me.

I rubbed my hand over the bump on my head. "Great," I sighed. "Now I'm hallucinating talking cats. Maybe I *have* got concussion."

I stared at the cat, waiting for it to meow or do something... well, cat-like.

Instead, it yawned lazily and stretched. "Oh please," it said, rolling its eyes. "If you're going to have a mental breakdown, at least make it interesting."

The cup I was holding clattered into the sink. "You... you can talk?" I stammered, feeling ridiculous even as I said it.

The cat fixed me with a patronising look. "I've always been able to talk," it said, flicking its tail. "But now you can understand me. Keep up, will you?"

I sank into the nearest chair, my legs suddenly weak. "But... how? Why?"

The cat sighed dramatically. "Listen closely, Josie, because I'm only going to explain this once. You're a witch. I'm your familiar. Surprise!"

I laughed. A nervous reaction rather than I found anything funny. "A witch? Me? Now I *know* I'm hallucinating."

"Says the woman having a conversation with a cat," it retorted. "Look, I know it's a lot to take in, but you have a very strong magical heritage. You're descended from the Stanton witches. Your grandmother was quite the powerhouse. And now you're fifty, it's your turn."

My mind reeled. Magic? Witches? Talking cats? I must have bumped my head harder than I thought.

"Why did I have to wait until I was fifty?" I asked, fixing on the least ridiculous part of the conversation.

The cat shrugged. "It's how things work with the Stanton witch line."

"So, what... I can do spells? Turn people into frogs?"

And I couldn't help thinking of Eva Henshaw.

The cat's whiskers twitched in amusement. "If you could turn someone into a frog right now, I'd be impressed. Magic has rules, and consequences."

I didn't like the sound of that.

"And you're... my magical guru?" I asked.

"Familiar," the cat corrected, looking slightly offended. "I'm here to assist you. And, in your case, to stop you doing spectacularly stupid things. I did try to warn you not to touch the clock, by the way, but no, you thought you knew better."

"Yeah, about that?" I said. "That clock gave me some kind of shock."

"Burst of magic," said the cat. "The clock does its own thing. It doesn't like to be touched."

"I figured that."

"And you were unconscious for hours," the cat added. "It's been years since your grandmother passed, and I was beginning to worry I'd have to wait for the next in line. A familiar's life can be quite boring without a witch." It glanced out of the window where two police officers were still poking around the greenhouse. "But you've really livened things up in the short time you've been here."

"Thanks...," I stuttered. "I think."

I rubbed my hand over my face. The swelling from earlier had almost disappeared.

"You've made a good job of healing yourself," the cat acknowledged.

"You think *I* did that?" I laughed.

"How else do you explain that you don't have concussion?"

I swallowed hard. The idea I might have somehow magically mended my own head was more unsettling than the fact I was having a conversation with a cat.

"OK, since you're my... familiar... perhaps you could explain a few things. Like could I use magic to, say, fix tiles on the roof? Or whip up a gourmet meal without actually cooking? I'm not great at that."

And I thought about Tom. Maybe I wouldn't be serving beans on toast after all.

The cat's eyes narrowed. "Ah, the inevitable 'how do I use magic for household chores' question. All newbie witches ask me that."

"How many have you known?" I asked.

"I've been in your family a looooong time," he said, stretching a paw to reveal sharp claws.

"Fine, so, no magical DIY or instant five-star dinners," I sighed, slightly disappointed. I looked at him. "Do you have a name?"

"Yes."

I waited.

"And your name is...?" I prompted.

"Not saying."

I was taken aback. "Why not?"

"Don't like it." He flicked his tail.

I laughed. "Well, calling you 'cat' seems a bit rude if we're going to be magical partners."

The cat's eyes narrowed. "If you even *think* about calling me any variation of 'Fluffy', I'll cough up a hairball in your shoe."

I held up my hands in surrender. "OK. Not Fluffy. How about... Shadow? Smokey? Midnight? Ooh, Obsidian? That's a great name."

"Too cliché."

"Merlin? Gandalf? Hercules? Amadeus?"

"Nope."

"Yoda?"

"Oh, come off the 'wise advisor' theme. I'm more than just your guide"

"Fine. you're a Persian, right? How about some Persian names? Danesh? Sitara?"

He eyed me. "How on earth do you know Persian?"

I shrugged. "I dated a guy obsessed with Persian poetry. He was rather boring, but I picked up some cool words." I sighed. "Oh, you *must* like one of these names. If you don't choose, I'm calling you Cutie Pie. Or Cuddlekins. Or..."

"Don't you dare."

I scratched my head. "OK, what about Salem? That's dark and mysterious and magical."

"That was my first name, given to me by the original Stanton sisters," he said. "But each new generation of witches has given me a new name."

"That must be confusing."

"Not for a cat of my intelligence."

I snapped my fingers. "Got it! Einstein."

The cat tilted his head, considering. "Hmm... intellectual, a touch eccentric, and known for his wild hair. There are worse comparisons. Yes. I like Einstein."

Through the window, I noticed another wave of police officers arriving at the greenhouse.

"Although, if I get arrested for murder, I don't suppose I'll be around long," I muttered.

Einstein's ears twitched. "Why would they arrest you?"

"The murder weapon. It's the candlestick I took off the mantelpiece. It has my fingerprints all over it."

Einstein blinked slowly, as though he needed to explain something that should be painfully obvious. "The candlestick you were planning to whack me with is still upstairs. The one that hit that obnoxious man was the doorstop in the greenhouse."

I started at him. "Why would anyone use a candlestick as a doorstop?"

"It's heavy."

"So's a rock."

Einstein fixed me with a hard stare. "All right, smarty pants. Originally, there were four matching candlesticks. One got broken, and Beatrix thought that three candlesticks on the mantelpiece looked unbalanced, so she put the third in the greenhouse. The one you brought upstairs is still on the bed, I passed it earlier. You can check if you want."

Relief flooded over me. At least I wasn't about to be hauled off in handcuffs.

However, Einstein was peering out of the window again. "Even so, you should probably figure out who *did* kill him. That would get rid of the police a lot faster."

"Me?" I snorted.

"I solved a murder with your grandmother once," said Einstein. "It was quite interesting."

I stared at him. "Are murders another part of 'normal' life in this house?" I asked. As if I hadn't already inherited enough unexpected baggage, now I had to worry about a legacy of killings too? "Is it cursed, or something?"

"Don't be ridiculous," scoffed Einstein. "That murder was in the village. But when faced with a mystery, your grandmother wasn't one to sit idly by and wait for the local constabulary to bumble their way to a solution."

"What are you suggesting?" I asked.

"I'm merely pointing out that the tools for the investigation are at your fingertips. The question is: will you use them?"

He stretched lazily before jumping down from the windowsill. "Look, I think it's time you attempted the library."

I glanced at my watch. "Won't the library be closed at this time of night?" I asked, not really fancying the idea of walking into Briarvale in the dark. "Do they open late or something?"

Einstein sighed heavily. "*Your* library, dummy."

Chapter 14

I**T WAS ALMOST DARK** now, and Einstein padded silently down the hallway, appearing and disappearing like a ghost as his dark shape crossed through the long shadows. The door to the library stood at the very end, partly hidden behind the staircase. Maybe that was why I'd missed it earlier.

"Here you go," said Einstein cheerfully. But as I took hold of the handle, he took a sharp intake of breath.

I instinctively pulled back at his reaction, the clock episode still fresh in my mind.

"Am I doing something wrong again?" I gasped.

"No, no, everything's fine... now," said Einstein. "Only a true descendant of the Stanton witches can open that door. You've just confirmed you're the real deal."

I peered at him. "What would've happened if I wasn't 'a true descendant'?"

Einstein's whiskers twitched. "Depends," he said. "It's funny, really. There was a locksmith who tried to open the door after your grandmother passed. You can see the scratches round the lock. He got the same reaction you got from the clock. Then there was a guy with an axe. He ended up in A&E. After that, people decided to leave the door alone."

"What!?" I gasped. "You could have mentioned that before I touched it."

"Would you have tried it?"

"Absolutely not."

"Thought so." He nudged the door open with a paw. "Shall we?"

I hesitated before stepping inside. The air shifted around me. It felt warm, full of the scent of old parchment and polished wood. This room was nothing like the rest of the house. No dust sheets. No cobwebs. Just towering bookshelves, a reading desk and a comfortable armchair, all bathed in a soft, golden glow that seemed to come from nowhere and everywhere at the same time.

"I love the smell of magic, don't you?" said Einstein, bounding into the room as pleased as though he'd grown two tails.

I wasn't sure what magic smelled like, but this room felt... different.

"It's been so long since I've been in here," Einstein purred contentedly.

The door closed behind us as if the library had a mind of its own.

"Now, if I remember rightly... and I always remember rightly... your grandmother left a letter for you." He leapt gracefully onto a nearby reading table. "Yes, here it is." He nosed at an envelope made from the same thick paper that had come with the deeds of the house. "You start reading, and I'll look for the diary where we solved that murder. It might help your current predicament. You can get to the grimoire and the recipe books some other time."

The letter from my grandmother was written in neat, careful handwriting.

My Dearest Josie,

If you're reading this, it means you've finally arrived at Briarwood Gables. I knew you'd come, my girl, as you were always meant to.

I entrust the house and estate to you, not just as its new custodian, but as the witch destined to carry forward our family's legacy. This place is not simply a house, it is your birth right. It knows you better than you know yourself.

The power that runs in the Stanton bloodline is subtle. Not the flashy spells of storybooks, but the deeper magic of understanding, of healing, of setting right what has gone wrong.

It breaks my heart that neither I nor your mother are here to help you, but I know our loyal friend and familiar will guide you. Please remember to fetch him a little catnip from time to time.

There is much I could tell you, but I won't. Not because I wish to keep things from you, but because you must discover them for yourself. We Stanton women have always been seekers. Our strength is not in what we inherit, but in what we uncover. There will be many surprises which you cannot yet explain. Do not be afraid of them. They are part of you, just as they were part of me.

You will find, as I did, that your sensitivity to the echoes imprinted on objects and places is both a gift and a responsibility. Use it wisely. Remember, magic works best when it serves justice and compassion, not personal gain. It isn't something that you do, it's something that you are.

Trust your instincts, and guard your heritage well, dear Josie.

One last thing, I left the house in the capable hands of Tom Carver. I knew he would care for it until your arrival. You may find you need him as much as he needs you.

Your loving Grandmother Beatrix

I had tears in my eyes when I finished reading. I felt so much love in the words. But Einstein was staring at me from a nearby shelf.

"I found the diary you need," he mewed, patting a thick leather-bound volume with his paw.

I walked over, pausing by the fireplace where a neat row of photographs had been placed. In varying degrees of age and fading, they showed generations of what I guessed were my ancestors - the Stanton witches.

"Come on, Josie," urged Einstein.

My hand hovered over the journal.

"Diaries are meant to be private, aren't they?"

"Your grandmother, like the other descendants of the Stanton witches, left her diary here to help future generations," Einstein insisted. "That means you."

A faint smell of lavender and something almost like cookie dough floated over me as I took it off the shelf.

"The murder investigation was around August time," Einstein told me. "Start there."

On the first page, written in an elegant swooping hand, were the words: 'Diary of Beatrix Pembroke, 14th Year of the Witch'.

I guess I must have looked confused because Einstein said, "Like you and all the Stanton Witches before you, she didn't come into her powers until her fiftieth year. This diary was written in the fourteenth year she was a witch."

"So she was sixty-four," I muttered. "She must have been experienced with magic."

"She was very comfortable with it," Einstein agreed.

I flicked through the book, passing entries detailing many, many visits to the village and countless hours spent in the kitchen. My grandmother seemed to do a *lot* of baking. She also had an endless stream of visitors eager to sample her creations.

"She loved her cooking," I remarked.

"Every witch likes cooking," said Einstein.

I grimaced. "Not this one."

"You'll learn," said Einstein.

I read through the diary entries. On 20th August, a murder shocked the village, which my grandmother solved with the help of Einstein and several batches of her honesty cookies.

"So, what do you think?" asked Einstein when I'd finished reading. "How do we solve the mystery of who murdered Graham Prescott by the greenhouse?" His amber eyes glinted expectantly.

""You know what, Einstein? I think it's time I embraced my heritage," I told him. "Tomorrow, I'll go into Briarvale to talk to the locals. And I'll need *you* to find me the recipe for my grandmother's honesty cookies."

Chapter 15

I HADN'T MEANT TO fall asleep in the library. My plan had been: head upstairs, pull the dust sheets off the bed in the room with the chintz curtains and the wardrobe full of clothes, and settle there for the night. But the chair was cosy and Einstein was still purring dreamily on my lap. Before I knew it, I was asleep.

By morning, Einstein had relocated to the windowsill, his grey fur gleaming in the sunlight streaming through the library window.

"Good morning, Sleeping Beauty," he drawled, stretching lazily.

I yawned, glancing round the room. So, everything yesterday hadn't been a dream.

"You've got the wrong fairy-tale," I told him. "I'm the witch, re-member?"

"True," said Einstein. "But 'good morning, Wicked Witch of the West' doesn't have the same vibe to it."

"I'm not a wicked witch!" I objected.

But Einstein just did that rumbling, purring laugh.

Shaking my head, I got up and headed for the kitchen. Einstein padded after me. Through the window, I spotted a lone police officer still stationed by the greenhouse. He gave me a small wave.

"Right," I said to Einstein as I filled the kettle. "Our murder investigation will start with that officer. I'll have a shower, and then we'll see what he can tell us."

Einstein regarded me with something that might have been approval. "I'm liking this new pro-active witch. Sleeping in the library can do that to you."

"It can do that to you?" I repeated slowly. I whirled round to look him in the eye. "You mean, the library has some sort of power, and you *planned* for me to sleep there? All that purring in my lap was a trick to lull me to sleep?"

Einstein looked like I'd accused him of secretly running a black-market tuna-smuggling gang. "Maybe," he drawled.

I wagged my finger at him. "You know, you are one sneaky cat."

Einstein jumped onto the windowsill. "I've been called worse," he said. "And look how well it worked. Today, you're all sunshine and positive vibes. Your grandmother would be proud of you."

A warm feeling spread through me. Suddenly, I wasn't annoyed any more. Sure, my life had been turned upside down, but for the first time in years, I felt a spark of excitement about the future. Of course, I'd need an income. Maybe the bed and breakfast idea was a good one.

"I hope she'd be proud," I said. "But no more of your tricks, right?"

Einstein started washing his paws and promised nothing.

As the kettle boiled, I made a jam sandwich courtesy of the Briarvale welcome committee, silently thanking my stars I hadn't thrown their offerings out after Eva and Florence told the police about my argument with Graham Prescott. Then, after a quick shower, I poured two cups of tea and took them outside.

The morning air was fresh and crisp as I stepped into the garden. Einstein followed me, jumping on the garden bench now glowing in golden sunlight.

"Good morning, Mrs Appleton," called the officer cheerfully, when he saw me approaching.

"Oh, call me Josie," I said.

The officer smiled. "Jamie," he told me. "Jamie Waverley."

This was going better than I'd hoped.

"Nice to meet you, Jamie." I offered him the second mug I carried. "I thought you might like some tea."

"Well, that is very kind of you," said Jamie, earnestly. "Thank you."

"No problem. I hope you haven't been here all night?" I asked.

Jamie took the cup. "Nah, I took over this morning. Once the DI confirms we've got all the evidence we need, I should be heading off." He took a sip of the tea and sighed. "Not that I'm in a rush. Your garden's beautiful. Peaceful."

"It is," I agreed. "That's all down to Tom. He's the one with the green fingers."

"Who's got green fingers?" said a voice behind me.

I turned to see Tom walking through the trees towards us. He was dressed in jeans and a blue t-shirt, his damp hair pushed back from his face. A pang of guilt hit me. Had he actually gone through with his plan of bathing in the river, rather than using the shower in the house? Einstein had been right: I *was* a wicked witch!

"Morning, Josie," Tom said cheerfully, as though he hadn't just endured a freezing swim because of me. He held out a box with several brown eggs inside. "Thought you might want some breakfast, courtesy of Hetty and Betty."

What? Now he was bringing me food after I'd treated him badly! I really was a wicked, wicked witch!

Tom gave me a cheeky grin. "That's presuming you know how to boil an egg, of course?"

I swallowed my guilt and mustered a smile. "Actually, I usually make a half decent job of scrambling eggs," I told him, taking the box. "Thank you for these."

"But are you good at scrambling *after* eggs?" quipped Jamie with a knowing grin. "I take it you'll both be going to the Runaway Egg Race tomorrow?"

For a moment, I didn't know what he meant, then I remembered the festival banners I'd seen in the village. "Umm, what's all that about?" I asked.

Jamie laughed. "The Runaway Egg Festival? It's the highlight of spring. Every year, the villagers get together and race to catch wooden eggs that are rolled down Briar Hill."

I looked at Tom. "Seriously?"

He grinned. "It's tradition."

"If I'm not mistaken," said Jamie, "Tom's caught an egg a couple of times?"

"I have," said Tom with a modest shrug.

I thought about Margot griping about her grandchildren's Easter egg hunt, and Barbara boasting about her expensive Easter lunch. Watching people chase wooden eggs down a hill sounded way more fun.

Jamie finished the last of his tea. "There used to be a woman lived here who always a had a stall at the Festival. She sold the most amazing cookies."

My ears pricked up at that. That sounded like the perfect opportunity to get people to eat honesty cookies, solve the murder and get the police out of Briarwood Gables.

"That would be my grandmother," I told him. "I have her recipe book. Maybe I could make cookies to sell too?"

Tom raised an eyebrow. "I thought you told me you were hopeless in the kitchen?"

"Baking cookies doesn't count," I told him firmly. "There's no chopping and peeling. And, let's be honest, anything tastes good with a sprinkling of sugar."

And in my head I added 'and magic', hoping that particular ingredient would make my efforts in the kitchen at least edible.

"Well, if you're half the baker that your grandmother was, I'm sure the villagers will love it." Jamie handed me his cup. "Thanks for the tea."

"Right," said Tom. "I'm off to repair a fence this morning over at the school. See you later."

"So, how's the investigation going?" I asked Jamie, as casually as I could.

Jamie hesitated a fraction before answering. "Well, you know how it is," he said, giving me a polite but noncommittal smile. "These things take time."

I smiled too. "I suppose you can't really say much."

"Not really," he admitted. "But I imagine you already know the basics: Graham Prescott took a nasty blow to the head, which we're treating as suspicious."

I nodded. "The candlestick?" I couldn't help but ask.

"Yes." Jamie must have noticed my expression because his tone softened. "I know it's a bad thing to happen in your garden but try not to worry. We'll get to the bottom of it. DI Holloway is very thorough."

I thought about the detective almost accusing *me* of hitting Prescott.

"Of course," I said, forcing a breezy tone. "Well, I appreciate the update. And at least you're getting to enjoy the garden while you're here."

Jamie chuckled. "That I am. And I have to say, this might be the best cuppa I've had on duty in a while."

I smiled, making a mental note to keep Jamie well-supplied with tea. He wasn't giving much away right now, but maybe next time?

Einstein suddenly trotted down the path. "You might want to wrap this up," he said in a low voice. "We've got company."

I spun round.

"Who?"

At first, I didn't see anything. Then, from the direction of the trees, a large, scruffy goat came trotting purposefully towards us, his horns low, his slitty green eyes locked onto Jamie like he was about to serve him a court eviction order.

Jamie must have sensed something too because he turned.

"Oh," he said. "You have a goat. That's nice."

"Run," Einstein advised.

I didn't need telling twice. I dashed for the door as Mr Tuppyhead broke into a full gallop.

"RUN!" I called over my shoulder to Jamie.

To his credit, Jamie bolted across the lawn with a surprising turn of speed as Mr Tuppyhead thundered after him, hooves kicking up clumps of grass. Jamie dodged left, then right, but Mr. Tuppyhead was relentless, chasing him in determined circles around the garden.

I watched, peering from the safety of the kitchen doorway. "Does the goat ever give up?" I asked Einstein.

"Not until he's made his point," chortled Einstein.

"And his point is?"

"Strangers shouldn't be in his garden."

Jamie made a desperate leap over a flowerbed, barely avoiding a well-aimed head butt, and with a final burst of speed he vaulted over the garden gate, landing on the other side with a grunt. Mr Tuppyhead skidded to a halt, let out a triumphant snort, then turned and trotted away, his mission evidently complete.

"Sorry," I called to Jamie.

Jamie straightened, dusted himself off, and adjusted his uniform. "Right," he said, breathless. "I might keep up my surveillance on the greenhouse from here, Mrs Appleton."

"Well, that was fun," said Einstein, purring round my legs. "What are we going to do next?"

I shut the door. "Now, we find a cookbook."

Chapter 16

Leaving the eggs Tom had given me in the kitchen, I set off for the library.

Einstein padded behind. "You know, I admire your optimism, which may be partly my fault due to the sleeping-in-the-library thing," he conceded. "But offering to bake cookies for the Runaway Egg Festival, when you've never done anything remotely magical, seems rather... ambitious, don't you think?"

"I healed my own head, remember?" I told him.

Einstein's eyes narrowed. "Yes, but we have no idea of the scope of your magical abilities. Baking is an exact science, and magical baking... well, let's say the consequences can be rather explosive."

"You mean like touching-the-clock-and-getting-blown-across-the-room-and-knocked-unconscious explosive?" I asked, suddenly feeling nervous.

"Possibly," said Einstein. "You have to follow the instructions to the letter and..."

"Well, that's where you come in," I said breezily. "Remember, it was you who wanted me to solve the murder, so don't be a killjoy."

Einstein still trailed behind me down the hallway.

"Hurry up," I insisted. "I need you to help me find the cookbook for the honesty cookies."

"Honesty cookies need advanced magic," he grumbled. "I don't think..."

"Well, I'll start with something easier," I interrupted. "*Then* I'll tackle the honesty cookies."

"But..."

"Oh, admit it, you're impressed by my magical enthusiasm," I teased.

Einstein's whiskers twitched in what might have been a reluctant smile. "Let's not get carried away. Though I suppose your determination is... not entirely unwelcome."

The scent of old books and magic sent a shiver down my spine as we entered the library. I scanned the shelves with awe. "OK. Where do I look?"

Einstein's tail twitched. "Third shelf from the top, second bookcase on the right. *The Witch's Grimoire of Enchanted Baked Delights.* That's a good place to start."

I retrieved the book and brought it to the reading table. The cover shimmered faintly under my fingers as I opened it, revealing pages filled with gentle watercolour illustrations and tiny, elegant script.

"Ooh, look at this!" I exclaimed, pointing at the first recipe. "Mood-Lifting Lemon Squares." I flicked over the pages. "Fortune-Telling Fruitcake, Tranquillity Thyme Loaf Cake, Self-Assured Strawberry Muffins!"

I squinted at the ingredients. "But I'm going to need a magnifying glass to read these." A grin spread across my face. "And I have one," I crowed. "Thank you, my London friends."

I fetched the magnifying glass from the tote. Its diamond encrusted rim seemed weirdly appropriate for reading magic spells. I pored over the instructions.

"These seem very detailed. How hard can it be?"

"Famous last words." Einstein sighed heavily. "Maybe you could start with the muffins, or the loaf cake. They're usually less of a disaster."

"Right. I'll make both of those," I agreed. "And I'll jot down the ingredients for the honesty cookies too, then I'll walk into town and buy everything I need."

But my enthusiasm faltered as I read down the list of ingredients. Alongside the normal things like flour, sugar and eggs were things like pixie dust and sunbeams.

I looked at Einstein. "Don't suppose there's a shop selling moon-water in the village?"

"Ha ha," chortled Einstein. "You don't *buy* moon-water," he choked. "You *infuse* moonbeams into water when the moon is full."

I scowled at him. "OK, smarty paws," I snapped. "But look." I pointed at the muffin recipe which called for two teaspoons of moon-water. "This is a setback. I don't even know when it's the next full moon."

Einstein stopped laughing. "You could always look in the storeroom," he said. "That's where we keep the herbs and hexes." And he trotted to the back of the room to a narrow door between two towering bookcases.

"Huh! I'll just go to the storeroom, should I?" I said, mimicking his smug manner as I followed him down the room.

I'd not really explored the library further than the armchair, and I hesitated before turning the doorknob.

"There's no chance this door has a magical defence mechanism for people it doesn't approve of?" I asked, suddenly nervous.

Einstein's whiskers twitched in amusement. "Only one way to find out, isn't there?"

Still I hesitated. "What exactly *am* I going to find in here? I hope there won't be bats flying around, or toads jumping on the floor."

Einstein started laughing again, so taking a deep breath, I turned the knob and pulled open the door. The room was small, and, thankfully, there were no bats or toads in sight. Instead, there were floor-to-ceiling shelves stocked to bursting with jars of colourful spices, bags of exotic powders, and bottles of mysterious essences.

"Oh my," I breathed, reaching out to touch a jar of what looked like glittering sugar. "Is this... fairy dust?"

"Pixie sugar," Einstein corrected, sounding bored. "Much less potent, thank goodness. We'd hate to have you accidentally shrinking the entire village."

I turned to him, my eyes wide with excitement. "Einstein, do you know what this means?"

He yawned dramatically. "That we're about to embark on a potentially disastrous baking adventure that ends with the fire brigade being called?"

I couldn't help but laugh. "No, you pessimistic furball. It means, I'm going to follow in my grandmother's footsteps, bake some cakes and solve who killed Graham Prescott. The Runaway Egg Festival won't know what hit it!"

"That's precisely what I'm afraid of," Einstein muttered.

Ignoring his doom and gloom, I ran my fingers along the jars. Powdered cobwebs, thistledown fluff...

"Of course, you'll still have to go and buy the flour and butter," Einstein pointed out.

"I know," I agreed. "But we're going to make the most magical cakes Briarvale has ever seen!"

"Heaven help us all," muttered Einstein. "Remind me never to let you sleep in the library again."

But nothing could dampen my spirits now. I had some of the cash left that I'd withdrawn in London. I had a storeroom full of magic, a book of enchanted recipes and an advisor cat. What could possibly go wrong?

Chapter 17

HALF AN HOUR LATER, armed with my list of ingredients, I sat in the hallway lacing up my boots. Next, I unloaded the tea-set out of my Fifty and Freaking Out tote onto the hall table, but I had barely settled the bag on my shoulder when a sharp rap on the front door echoed through the house.

DI Holloway and Officer Chen stood on the doorstep. "Good morning, Mrs Appleton," the DI said, in a tone that suggested it might not be.

I straightened up. "Umm, good morning," I said warily.

His eyes locked on to me, dark and intimidating. "Interesting timing, wouldn't you say? You arrive in Briarvale, and within hours, there's a murder on your doorstep."

I swallowed hard. "I hardly think my moving here has anything to do with Mr Prescott's death."

"And then there's your husband. I hear he's disappeared under, shall we say, unusual circumstances."

My chest tightened. DI Holloway had clearly been doing his homework.

"Gary has nothing to do with any of this," I snapped.

"Is that so?" Holloway mused. "Because it does make one wonder. Mr Appleton ran a property business, like Graham Prescott. Maybe *he* had a reason to want Prescott out of the way. Maybe your husband didn't disappear at all. Maybe he's hiding right here in Briarvale." He let the words hang in the air.

I sucked in a sharp breath. "That's ridiculous. Gary doesn't even know about Briarwood Gables. I didn't know about it myself until two days ago."

"Convenient timing," noted Holloway. "Maybe you killed Mr Appleton and Prescott saw, so you killed him, too?" he suggested.

For a moment, I was too stunned to speak. "Of course I didn't kill Gary." My voice rose to a squeak. "And I didn't kill Graham either."

There was another silence while we stared at each other.

"Still, husbands don't usually vanish into thin air," said Holloway at last.

I narrowed my eyes. "No, they don't. Most men don't spectacularly bankrupt their wives and flee the country either, but yet, here we are."

A muscle twitched at the corner of Holloway's eye. "Touchy subject?" he asked, as if he'd just proven a point.

I clenched my teeth. "What exactly are you implying, Detective?"

"Merely making observations, Mrs Appleton." His gaze flicked to the tote bag slung over my shoulder. "Going somewhere?"

"Briarvale. Shopping."

There was another pause, then his voice hardened. "Do yourself a favour, Mrs Appleton. Don't leave town." And with that, he and Chen turned and walked back to his car.

I let out a slow breath, hoping my heart didn't hammer its way out of my chest.

Einstein threaded himself around my legs. "The detective's really clutching at straws," he said. "He must have no clue who the killer is."

"He clearly hasn't," I agreed. "Which makes it all the more urgent that we solve this case before he arrests me so that he can get his paperwork out of the way."

My fingers were still shaking as I adjusted the tote bag on my shoulder.

"Alright," I told the freaking-out woman. "We're normal, non-magical, definitely-not-murder-suspects going on a totally ordinary hike to the shop. Bet you never expected all this adventure when you landed on this city girl's birthday list."

The half-mile walk to Briarvale stretched before me, a winding country lane between hedgerows bursting with primroses and bluebells. The scent of damp earth and wildflowers drifted on the breeze and birds chattered noisily in the trees.

"Remember, we're after supplies, and clues to the murderer," I said, more to myself than I thought Einstein might need the reminder.

Einstein's tail flicked. "Try not to hex anyone by accident."

"Ha ha," I replied, sticking out my tongue. "You know I have no idea how to do that."

"No, but you didn't know how to heal your head yesterday, and you don't even have a mark now," said Einstein ominously.

I ignored the shiver that ran down my spine and pressed onwards. At the top of a small hill, I felt a flutter of excitement as the thatched roofs and the church spire came into view. We walked past a neat, whitewashed bungalow, then a large grey house before reaching the humpback bridge which arched over Briar Brook. I stopped, leaning over the parapet. Below, the water burbled happily, so clear you could see tiny fish darting between the pebbles at the bottom.

Einstein jumped up onto the wall beside me.

"Hey, no fishing today," I told him.

"As if," he said, neatly picking his way along the edge.

But sightseeing would have to wait for another day. I continued to the main street and made a beeline for Fletcher's Fine Goods Store.

I expected Einstein to follow me inside, but instead, he hopped onto a bench outside the shop, curling his tail neatly around himself.

"You're on your own with this one," he declared. "Mr Fletcher says it's unhygienic to have cats in food shops. He used to throw me out. Rather disagreeable man."

I raised an eyebrow. "And that was enough to put you off?"

"Of course not," Einstein sniffed. "But the man has an excellent aim with a broom."

I laughed as Einstein settled on the bench, took a deep breath, and went inside the shop solo.

It was dark inside Fletcher's Fine Goods, but the air was a delightful mix of beeswax, vanilla and aromatic spices, and there was the cheerful sound of someone humming a slightly off-key version of 'Hit the Road, Jack' close by.

Once my eyes adjusted to the dim light, I took in the charming hodgepodge of old and new, with gleaming jars of hand-labelled preserves sitting alongside bars of trendy, eco-friendly snacks.

"Well, if it isn't Briarvale's newest resident," a warm voice called out.

I turned to see a man peering at me from behind the counter, his round glasses perched precariously on his nose. If this was Edwin Fletcher, he didn't look disagreeable to me.

"You got me," I said with a smile.

The man chuckled. "Name's Fletcher. Edwin Fletcher."

For a second, I thought I'd walked into a James Bond movie. "Appleton," I replied. "Josie Appleton."

We both laughed. Definitely not disagreeable. Maybe he just didn't like cats.

"I'm here to stock up," I told him. "I hope you have plenty of flour and sugar."

"Sounds like you inherited the baking gene from your grandmother," said Edwin approvingly. "Beatrix always had something tasty tucked inside her basket." And he eyed the tote bag hopefully.

Oh boy, no pressure. How was I going to live up to her reputation? I really hoped the magic cookbooks would help.

"I doubt I'm as good as she was," I admitted.

"I'm sure you're being modest," Edwin told me. He pointed a finger. "The baking section's along the back wall."

I pulled my shopping list out of my pocket and wandered along the shelves. Einstein had told me Beatrix always tripled the ingredients of her recipes, and I wanted to make sure I had enough to give out at the Runaway Egg Festival. This meant I almost cleared Fletcher's store out of flour, and my bag weighed a ton.

No matter. This was not something that could be skimped on.

I picked up sugar and butter, and then added a loaf of bread and a couple of tins of beans on top. They would do for me to eat later. I planned on buying a sandwich at the HoneyPot Tearoom so I could pick up any clues there. And, as I'd be back in the village tomorrow for the festival, I could buy the other things I needed then.

I hauled my shopping to the counter. Now I needed to find out if Edwin knew anything about Graham Prescott.

Chapter 18

"I SUPPOSE YOU HEARD about the murder at Briarwood Gables," I ventured casually, as Edwin rung my shopping through the till.

He nodded, but instead of looking grim, an odd smile played round his mouth. "Shocking business," he said, but there was a lightness in his tone. Something I couldn't put my finger on. Relief, maybe?

"I only met him one time," I said, watching Edwin's reaction carefully. "Did you know Graham Prescott well?"

Edwin's lips pursed as if he'd bitten into a lemon. "Well enough." He picked up a bag of flour. "Prescott wasn't the most pleasant of customers." He paused. "Let's say he had a talent for rubbing people the wrong way with his big ideas and fancy schemes. He thought he could bulldoze his way through this village, and we were supposed to stand aside and let him, but you can only push people so far before..." He stopped and cleared his throat. "Well, before they get fed up with it." He dropped the flour into my tote bag with more force than was probably necessary. "The village... no, the world... is better off without Graham Prescott," Edwin finished.

Wow, that got a reaction. Had Graham pushed Edwin to his limit? But surely this apparently pleasant grandad wasn't the candlestick-wielding type? And what would be his motive?

I paid, then heaved my bag onto my shoulder and went to find Einstein, leaving Edwin humming 'I Can See Clearly Now'.

"Solved the murder yet?" Einstein asked, swatting idly at an ant running along the back of the bench.

"Edwin didn't like Graham," I reported.

"Edwin didn't like *me*," Einstein pointed out. "And no-one liked Graham." He eyed the tote bag. "That looks heavy. Think it'll last the journey home?"

"Hey, us 'fifty and freaking out' types can handle a shopping bag full of cake ingredients," I huffed. "But first, we'll nip into the HoneyPot and see if we can pick up any clues there."

Einstein jumped down from the bench. "Because nothing says 'solving crimes' like a sugar rush and the caffeine jitters."

"I take it you're actually coming inside the HoneyPot with me?" I asked Einstein as we walked along the street.

"Oh yes," he purred. "Sylvia loves me."

The cheerful jingle of the doorbell announced our arrival. The tearoom was bustling, with a group of noisy hikers filling the tables at the back, and an elderly couple sitting in the middle eating scones.

"Morning, Josie love!" Sylvia called, handing some warm pastries to a woman with walking boots and a rucksack. "Come in."

I waited while the hiker paid.

"Oh, my goodness," said Sylvia. "You have a cat. Beatrix had a cat that followed her, too." She peered at Einstein. "You know, if I didn't know better, I'd swear it was exactly the same one."

Einstein started that purring laugh. "Because I *am* exactly the same one," he chuckled.

"But that would make him impossibly old for a cat," Sylvia was saying.

I couldn't help but smile. "I found this cutie pie at the house," I told her.

"Cutie pie?" spat Einstein, his ears going flat.

"Maybe he's an offspring of my grandmother's cat," I said by way of explanation of his identical appearance.

"Smooth lie," said Einstein approvingly.

"Think he'd like a lick of cream?" Sylvia asked. "Your grandmother's cat did."

Einstein answered for himself with a particularly loud, long, drawn out meow.

"So, what can I get for you?" Sylvia asked, setting a saucer on the floor for him.

I surveyed the counter. "I'd like a coffee and one of your cheese salad baguettes... and a cake... but I can't decide which one. They all look so nice."

Sylvia laughed. "I would recommend the lemon drizzle cake," she said. "That can solve most of life's problems."

"In that case, definitely the lemon drizzle," I laughed.

After I'd paid, I headed for the table by the window. This was becoming my regular seat. Einstein hopped onto the sill beside me.

"I've not been in here since your grandmother passed," he told me. "It's good to be back."

While I tucked into my baguette, the hikers bought more cake to go, and they piled out, raucously shouting their thanks to Sylvia. No sooner had they gone than the bell over the door jangled again, and Terry Grady stepped into the HoneyPot, bringing with him a gust of cool air and a face like thunder.

"What can I get you, Terry?" Sylvia asked.

"Coffee and a ham sandwich, please," Terry muttered, barely meeting her eye.

I didn't mean to eavesdrop, but there's something about a quiet tearoom and a disgruntled builder that makes it impossible not to.

"You alright, Terry, love?" Sylvia asked. "You seem a bit... off."

Terry let out a heavy sigh and rubbed a hand over his face. "Honestly, Sylv, I don't know what to do," he admitted, his voice husky and choked. "The last time I saw Prescott he was all apologetic about the Polvarren care home job. He *promised* he'd hire me to work on the health spa. Swore on his life. And I thought, 'finally, a decent job'." He shook his head. "I thought the spa would be good for the village. I even stuck my neck out and helped him win people around to the scheme; went to the planning meetings and everything. I mean, there was only me and Edwin that were in favour when we started, but we talked everyone into it. And then what happens? They bring in a bunch of contractors from out of town and cut me out... again."

Terry's fists were clenched at his sides.

"At this rate, I'll be out of business before the summer," he groaned.

"Oh, I'm sorry, love," said Sylvia, sliding his coffee over the counter. "I'm sure something'll turn up."

Terry let out a hollow laugh. "Yeah, well. Lesson learned. If you trust the wrong person, you end up with nothing."

I thought about Gary. I had to agree with Terry on that.

Terry picked up the coffee and stared at it. "Still, I guess Prescott finally ran out of people to screw over. You can't stab people in the back when you're face down in the dirt. He got what he had coming in the end, and good riddance."

I stopped, my coffee cup hovering just below my lips. Terry was more than angry, he was furious.

Was he furious enough to kill Graham Prescott?

Terry Grady had just made his way to the top of my suspect list.

After Terry had left the shop, Sylvia took a moment to join me and Einstein at our table.

"So, how are you settling in, love?" she asked.

I shrugged. "It was all going fine... until Graham Prescott turned up... well, you know."

Sylvia reached across the table and patted my hand. "It was an awful thing to happen."

I nodded towards the door. "Terry didn't like Prescott."

"Not many round these parts did," Sylvia admitted. "Graham had a knack for making enemies faster than I can whip up a Victoria sponge."

I hesitated. "I've just been in Fletcher's store. Edwin wasn't a fan either."

Sylvia frowned. "Funny thing with Edwin," she said. "Prescott was always in his shop like they were best buddies, but his death doesn't seem to have affected Edwin at all. In fact, when I popped in earlier, he was singing 'Happy Days Are Here Again'."

"He was singing when I went in, too," I told her.

Sylvia nodded towards my tote bag. "Stocking up, I see. I hope all this trouble hasn't put you off staying."

I didn't know how to answer that. In the course of a few days, I'd gone from bankrupt deserted housewife, to witch, to murder suspect. But Graham Prescott had no shortage of enemies, and if I didn't figure out which one had finally had enough of him, my future was as uncertain as ever.

My best hope? Magical baking.

And there was a sentence I never thought I'd think.

Chapter 19

THE FREAKING-OUT WOMAN ON my tote bag almost sighed with relief when I dumped it onto the table after our hike home. She had certainly lost a lot of sparkle during our walk, and so had I. I collapsed onto a chair, groaning as I circled my aching shoulders.

"I need a car," I muttered. But that would drain my bank account, assuming I still had one, faster than I could say 'monthly payments'.

"Maybe Edwin does home delivery?" I muttered.

Einstein seemed unaffected by our trek into the village. He jumped on the table beside me. "You need to get baking," he reminded me. "You should have walked faster. It's already the middle of the afternoon."

"Shut up," I grumbled, waving him away, but all the same, I dragged myself to my feet and picked up the kettle.

As I turned on the tap, I was surprised to see Jamie Waverley still stationed by the greenhouse. DI Holloway obviously hadn't given up on the crime scene. The thought turned my stomach.

"No use worrying about that now," I told Einstein, unloading the non-magical ingredients from the bag.

I fetched my grandmother's recipe book from the library, turning the page to Tranquillity Thyme Loaf Cake. The key magical ingredient was listed as 'a pinch of serenity'.

"What's that?" I asked Einstein.

"Red jar in the storeroom," he told me.

The jar wasn't hard to find. It glowed faintly on the shelf. That was handy.

I unscrewed the top. A faint smell of lavender and honey drifted out.

"How much is a pinch?" I wondered.

Einstein flicked his tail. "Enough to take the edge off, but not so much you turn Briarvale's residents into blissed-out zombies."

"Not super helpful," I muttered, heading back to the kitchen with the jar.

Einstein patted a cupboard near the oven. "Bowls, weighing scales, baking trays are all in here," he told me, like he was overseeing a particularly hopeless student.

He fussed over measuring ingredients, made me mix until my arms ached, and supervised setting the temperature for the oven to the precise degree. But when it came to adding the serenity powder, he jumped in front of me.

"Wait," he instructed. "First, you have to take several deep breaths."

I looked at him, the jar of powder in my hand. "Seriously?"

"Do I look like I'm joking?"

"No," I sighed.

"Stop! Not a breath like that," he chastised. "That was frustration. Now you'll have to start again. You need to breathe. Release all tension, or the magic won't work."

"But I feel stupid," I squirmed.

"And you'll feel even more stupid if your baking turns out cursed," he scolded me. "How about you sit down first? Look, you never finished your tea. Maybe that would help."

Obediently, I sat at the table. My drink had gone cold, but I sipped it anyway.

"I expected to be chanting rhymes and waving wands," I told him.

"Not necessary for loaf cake," he told me. He jumped on my lap and settled down, a deep, steady purr running through me. After a minute, I felt calmer.

"You're a good assistant," I told him, scratching behind his ears.

"I know," he replied smugly.

Once Einstein decided I was sufficiently relaxed, I was finally allowed to sprinkle in the serenity powder and slide the loaf cakes into the oven.

"You might want to alert the fire brigade to be on standby," he teased.

"Don't be cheeky," I told him, dusting flour off my hands and flipping to the recipe for Self-Assured Strawberry Muffins.

It had taken nearly two hours to mix the loaves. If I didn't get a move on, I'd be baking all night.

The muffins required moon-water, and Einstein directed me to a small blue bottle in the storeroom.

"Your grandmother infused this water before she died, so it's been sitting on the shelf a long time. I hope it still has some strength," he said.

"The recipe calls for two teaspoons, so maybe we should add three?" I suggested. "To be on the safe side?"

Einstein scratched his ear, considering the matter. "Not an entirely terrible idea," he agreed. "And we'll bottle some fresh at the next full moon."

Mixing the batter went smoothly enough. The moon-water was the last ingredient.

"Now," said Einstein, as I picked up the teaspoon. "Look in the jar and say, 'I am capable. I am strong. I will not burn the muffins'."

"Really?" I rolled my eyes. "I am capable," I muttered. "I am..."

"Say it like you mean it," Einstein interrupted. "Start again."

It took six attempts before Einstein was satisfied. Finally, I measured the moon-water and stirred it in with as much confidence as I could muster.

"Speaking of burning," said Einstein suddenly, sniffing the air, "you should check on the loaf cakes."

I shot to the oven. Sure enough, the tops were beginning to crisp, but they were golden and brown, and they smelled delicious as, under Einstein's instruction, I tipped them onto my grandmother's cooling trays.

"Those look half decent," Einstein admitted grudgingly.

"I should try one," I said, reaching for a knife.

"Noooooo!" Einstein yowled. "Taking your own magic is a terrible idea."

I looked at the loaves disappointedly. "Fine, I'll put the muffins in, and then I'll eat my beans on toast before tackling the honesty cookies."

I'd been so focussed on baking, I'd almost forgotten about the police in my garden, but as I opened the can of beans, I noticed there were now three officers. One was lifting a flagstone in the path.

What on earth were they doing this time?

I thought back to my earlier trip into the village. Graham Prescott had made no shortage of enemies. Edwin Fletcher didn't like him, and Sylvia had noticed how cheery Edwin had been in the last few days

- the days since Graham had been found dead. But what motive did Edwin have to kill him?

Terry Grady had motive, but unless I could prove otherwise, he'd been going to a job in Trevenna on the morning of the murder. That was something I could check, if I knew what job he'd been quoting for.

But whoever had killed Graham had had the nerve to come into my garden, pick up a candlestick and hit him. What had they been doing on my property? And my mind turned to Tom again. I watched the officers poking about under the flagstone. Had Graham, or whoever killed him, buried something in my garden? I needed to find out.

"I'll take the police a drink and ask what they're doing," I told Einstein. "Maybe some loaf cake would help."

Einstein's ears flattened to his head. "I'm not sure trying out your first attempt at a spell on officers of the law is a good plan."

Chapter 20

I LOOKED FROM EINSTEIN to the loaf cake. "It *looks* fine," I said. "And I really need to know what's happening."

Confidently, I cut some slices and arranged them on a plate. But as I carried the tea and cakes outside, DI Holloway pulled up the drive.

"Mrs Appleton," he remarked, glowering at the tray in my hands. "This is a crime scene, not a café."

"I'm sorry," I stammered. "I was just being polite." I looked at the flagstone the officers had lifted which now lay on the soil at the side of the path. "Why are you digging up my paving?"

"You seem awfully interested in what my officers are doing," Holloway noted. "Is there something you're worried we might find?"

"Of course not." I said, heat creeping up my neck. "I was actually wondering whether I would get compensation for all the damage your officers are causing to my garden."

"Don't worry, Josie, we'll put...," Jamie Waverley started, but DI Holloway silenced him with a stern look.

"Well, I'll leave these here in case you get peckish later," I huffed, putting the tray on the grass, while secretly hoping Mr Tuppyhead would come and chase the detective back to his car. Unfortunately, the goat was nowhere to be seen.

Back inside, I warmed up the can of beans. It was a poor meal after the stew Tom had made the night before, and no sooner had I sat down than Einstein declared the muffins should be ready, so I had to get up again to take them out of the oven.

I admit, I didn't feel like setting into baking again. The last few days had taken their toll on me, and I yawned as I set the dishes in the sink.

"Are you *sure* there isn't a spell to magically deal with the washing up?" I asked Einstein.

"Absolutely not," he said bluntly.

"Right. Back to baking then," I sighed.

I picked up a packet of flour and was about to pour some into my mixing bowl when Einstein launched himself across the table and batted the bag out of my hand.

"That's plain flour!" he yowled. "Your cookies would be all flat."

With a pounding heart, I picked up a different packet. "That was some tackle," I spluttered.

Einstein went back to licking a paw. "You're welcome."

"But you could have just said, 'Josie, you have the wrong flour'. You didn't have to go full ninja on the bag."

"Trust me, on a scale of 'bad idea' to 'full-blown magical catastrophe', rugby tackling the bag was the best damage control I had," Einstein purred.

"Alright, hero cat," I laughed. "I've got the right stuff this time."

The instructions were simple: standard cookie ingredients plus a drop of veritas extract.

Easy.

I found the bottle in the storeroom. The liquid inside shimmered like molten silver.

"Careful with that," Einstein warned. "Too much and people will overshare in ways you don't want to hear. Oh, and don't breathe the fumes as you pour. Just a sniff will have an effect."

Carefully holding my breath, I dropped a single drop into the dough. The cookies looked perfect going into the oven. Now I needed to clean up.

Einstein curled up on a chair and shut his eyes, but I'd barely started running the water when Kim rang.

"You look busy," she said.

"I'm baking," I told her.

There was a silence. "Mum, when do you ever bake?" Kim asked. Then she laughed. "Remember the cake you made for my ninth birthday? Dad used it as a doorstop."

I cringed. "It lasted for years," I admitted.

Kim's eyes narrowed. "Speaking of my dad, I tried to call him today. I got a message saying his number has been disconnected."

I put down the mixing spoon, steeling myself for telling her what was happening. "Ah... Yes... There's something I need to talk to you about."

Kim looked at me expectantly.

I took a deep breath. "Well, you see..."

"Nana!" interrupted Ivy, her freckled face beaming. "I can do a cartwheel at gymnastics: a really good one. Watch this."

Kim turned the phone round so I could see Ivy tossing round the living room, and then Juno arrived to join in. Eventually, Kim sent the twins into the garden to practise.

"So?" she said. "What's really happening?"

"Well," I started. "On my birthday..."

But then Kim let out a screech. "Mum! Behind you!"

I turned. A thick, black cloud puffed from the oven, and a distinctly unpleasant smell was starting to fill the room. "Oh my goodness!" I gasped. "Look Kim. I may need the fire brigade. I'll speak to you tomorrow. Love you."

Coughing, I yanked the tray out of the oven. The cookies had expanded into monstrous, cracked lumps with a strange, shiny, silver surface that released a puff of green something I didn't want to breathe in as I dropped them onto the top of the cooker.

I took a cautious step backwards.

"Oh, that's not good," screeched Einstein, retreating to the door-way.

I didn't need telling twice. "Well, they didn't go flat," I coughed, before grabbing the tray and launching the whole mess out through the window.

Einstein wrinkled his nose. "Too much veritas extract. Those aren't cookies, Josie. They're truth grenades waiting to explode. If those things start talking, I want no part in this."

"Oh, don't tell me they talk!" I groaned. I dashed to the window, peering into the darkness.

A low, whispery voice rose from the pile of ruined cookies. "Lies! Deception! Betrayal!"

I stared in horror. But that wasn't even the worst part. A white goose was pecking at them with disturbing enthusiasm.

"Nooo!" I shot to the door, dishcloth in hand. Tom had told me Agatha liked shiny things. Goodness knows what eating a tray full of silvery, burnt honesty cookies would do to her.

"Shoo!" I shouted, waving my dishcloth like a wild thing. "No! Bad goose."

"Everything alright, Mrs Appleton?"

DI Holloway had gone. Now there was only one police officer left. He was sitting on a fold-up chair inside the greenhouse with the empty plate of loaf cake on his knee, and an amused grin on his face.

"Fine," I called back, trying to sound like a respectable member of society who wasn't swiping at a goose with a dishcloth. At least my baking hadn't poisoned either of them... yet.

Agatha snatched up two more honesty cookies before I could grab the tray and deposit the rest into the bin. I slammed the lid shut, but a muffled, eerie voice echoed "Hon-nest-yyyyy" from within.

Honking like a demented car horn, Agatha began to circle the bin, clearly annoyed that I had stolen her prize.

"Agatha!"

Tom appeared from the direction of his caravan. "Go get her, Murphy."

The collie streaked towards me, herding the flapping, squawking goose away.

"Everything OK, Josie?" said Tom. He wafted at the smell of burning still lingering in the night air. "Something smells... uh... a bit cremated."

I sighed. "Told you I wasn't good at cooking."

Tom laughed. "So, I'm guessing you're not taking any baking to the festival tomorrow?"

"Oh, but I am," I told him proudly. "Not *everything* got burned."

"Then I'll look forward to sampling something," said Tom with a grin.

He glanced over to where Murphy was still wrangling a very voluble Agatha away from the house. Whatever the cookies she'd stolen might be making her confess, it was a good thing no-one understood Goose.

"I should go and help, Murph," Tom said. "Sounds like Agatha's got one on her tonight."

He disappeared into the trees, and I turned to go into the house when a loud snoring made me stop. The officer was now propped against the door jamb, head back, snoring like an express train.

Maybe the man was simply tired, and his falling asleep had nothing to do with loaf cake or magic. And I crossed my fingers tightly as I tiptoed over. I picked up the tray, leaving him to his slumbers, and went back to the house.

Einstein gave me a long, unimpressed look as I shut the door. "He's asleep, isn't he?" he asked.

I nodded.

"Looks like you put too much serenity powder in," he noted. "And that is why rookie witches stick to baking muffins."

I looked at the half bag of flour which remained on the table. "I don't have enough to try another batch of honesty cookies," I said, defeated. "And I *really* wanted to use them to find Graham Prescott's killer."

Einstein hopped onto the table, curling his tail around himself. "Probably for the best," he purred. "But on the bright side, the loaf cake and muffins smell like they're meant to. You're going to be a hit at the festival."

Chapter 21

S UNLIGHT STREAMED THROUGH THE curtains, far brighter than it should be at... I squinted at my phone...

Nine o'clock

No!

I hadn't meant to oversleep. But, staying up into the early hours scrubbing my baking mess off every surface in the kitchen and scraping strange silver particles out of the oven from the spoiled honesty cookies had taken its toll. Not to mention I'd spent the last two nights either slumped in the library chair or dozing on a train, so sleeping in a real bed in the cosy, striped pyjamas I'd found in a drawer had been heaven.

Today was the day of the festival. The day I'd put my magical baking to the test and hopefully figure out who really killed Graham Prescott.

I took the world's fastest shower, pulled on a clean pair of trousers and a dusky grey sweater sprinkled with tiny silver stars, and headed downstairs.

"You're cutting it fine," commented Einstein. He was perched on the windowsill, washing his whiskers like he had all the time in the world. "You still need to slice the rest of the loaf cake and wrap it. Your grandmother kept some flowery napkins in the bottom drawer for that purpose. And make sure you cut the pieces small. We don't want everyone as relaxed as the police officer you tried it on last night. If they all nod off before the Egg Race, the whole festival will be a disaster. Oh, and you need to find a way to carry everything into Briarvale. And you've not even had breakfast yet."

I glared at him. "Less judgement, more helpfulness," I muttered, peering past him at the greenhouse.

Thankfully, the snoring policeman had woken up. He didn't appear to have suffered any magical side-effects that I could see, and was pacing along the path slapping his hands together like he was trying to stay warm. Or stay awake. Or both.

Coming towards the house was Tom, with Murphy trotting at his heel.

Tom tapped at the kitchen door. "I was going to ask if you wanted a lift to the festival?"

"Oh, that would be a lifesaver," I said. "But I've not packed up my baking yet."

"No rush," Tom told me. "I'll meet you at my pickup in, say, an hour? I've got things to set up there, so I need to be early."

"That'll be perfect." I hesitated. "Was... umm... Agatha OK last night?"

Tom scratched his head. "Oh, that goose drove me mad," he said. "She made a noise non-stop. Kept following me around honking, looking all... well, guilty. Honestly, if I didn't know better, I'd say she was confessing her sins." He laughed. "And Agatha's got quite a criminal record when it comes to petty theft."

I forced a laugh. "Huh. Weird."

Weird didn't even begin to cover it. But at least she was OK.

Just under an hour later, I was wedging two boxes of magical cakes onto the front seat of Tom's truck. Einstein jumped up on top like a furry chaperone.

"Hey, the Fluffball's coming," commented Tom.

He'd changed into a red check shirt and black jeans and was looking unusually smart.

"That cat used to follow your grandmother everywhere," he told me. "But he hasn't set a paw outside the garden since she passed, and now here he is. Funny, he doesn't look a day older than when I first came to live here, but he must be ancient by now."

"Ancient indeed!" Einstein sniffed. "And why would I follow you? You're not a witch."

"Yes, he's really taken to me," I said, glad that Tom couldn't understand what Einstein had said.

As I squeezed in beside the cake boxes, a chorus of chaotic quacking erupted from the back. I twisted round to see two ducks in a wooden crate with Murphy standing proudly beside them.

"Tom!" I gasped. "Why are you taking ducks?"

"Bonnie and Clyde are here to help Murphy," he told me cheerfully. "He's making his debut this afternoon."

"Your dog has a stage career?" I asked, puzzled.

"Duck herding," said Tom, as though that explained everything. "We've been training for months. Today's his first public appearance."

"Duck herding," I repeated. "Right. And *I'm* the weird one for bringing a cat."

Einstein's tail twitched. "Mark my words, this is how it starts," he said. "First, it's ducks. Next, it'll be sheep in waistcoats. The world has gone mad."

The sun was high, the breeze was fresh, the birds were singing, the brook was babbling. The pickup rattled over the bridge and the village square came into view. My jaw dropped. The sleepy little hamlet I'd arrived in only days ago had been transformed into a bustle of activity. Colourful stalls lined the village green, their owners unpacking an array of homemade goods. The air buzzed with laughter, gossip, and the occasional clatter of dropped bakeware.

I'd never seen anything like this in London.

"Welcome to the madness," said Tom, pulling his truck in opposite the HoneyPot. Sylvia had several tables set outside the tearoom and she waved at us cheerily.

Tom unloaded the crate containing Bonnie and Clyde, setting it in the shade of a huge tree, and I jumped out of the truck.

"No, no, NO!" A shrill voice cut above the din.

I recognised it immediately.

Ugh! Eva Henshaw.

"The honey stall should *obviously* be on the left of the wood carvings," Eva scoffed, jabbing at the clipboard she was holding with a pen. "It's all here on the plan. And can someone *please* straighten that tablecloth. We have our standards, you know."

"That you do," I muttered, remembering how she had sold me out to the police. "And they're spectacularly low."

Eva was flanked by none other than the immaculately-dressed station master, Percy Henshaw. The same man I'd seen sweeping Briarvale Station with military precision the day I arrived.

Of course, Eva and Percy would be a couple. They were a perfect match.

Spoiling Percy's composure was Charlie, Eva's miniature dog, who was about to cock his leg on the corner of the wood carvings stall.

"Charlie! No!" Percy hissed, scooping him off the ground in the nick of time.

"Percy! Must you manhandle him like that?" Eva swept Charlie from his arms and cradled him like a baby. "Oh, poor little shoochikins," she cooed. "Did the nasty man interrupt your call of nature?"

Charlie gave a little yip and licked her face.

Yuk!

Two steps behind Eva as usual was Florence with her habitual worried expression, notebook in hand.

Eva came to a halt in front of me. "I didn't expect to see *you* here," she said. "I would have thought you would be busy with the murder investigation."

"And the cleaning," added Florence in a squeak

"Oh, I thought the festival was more important," I countered, meeting their gaze. "I understand my grandmother always contributed, and I wanted to carry on the tradition." I gestured to the boxes in Tom's pickup. "I was up most of the night baking," I said.

"That's nice," ventured Florence, but Eva shot her a look. "Or, maybe not," she stuttered. "I don't know."

"Would you like to try something?" I asked, heaving one of the boxes towards me along the seat of the truck.

"Not for me," Eva huffed. "I'm watching my diet. Doctor's orders."

I couldn't imagine Eva taking orders from anyone, but I held my tongue.

"Can I?" asked Florence.

"If you must," said Eva impatiently.

I bristled. Florence shouldn't have to ask Eva for permission to eat.

"Might I suggest a strawberry muffin?" I said, leaving out the 'self-assured' part. If anyone needed a boost in that department, it was Florence.

Charlie growled as I offered the box of strawberry muffins towards Florence.

"Oh, thank you," said Florence. She devoured the cake as though Eva might change her mind and take it off her at any moment. "They're really nice."

"Then have another," I pressed.

From his seat in the pickup, Einstein twitched his ears. "Now we're in for some fun."

Chapter 22

I PATTED MY BOX of baked goods. "Actually, I was hoping to sell these cakes. Is there a stall available?"

Eva's eyes narrowed, scanning the bustling square. "All full up, I'm afraid. Pity. It looks like your time was wasted baking all those cakes."

"But I don't need much room," I protested.

Tom left the crate of ducks and came over. "No worries," he said. "I'll drop the tailgate on the truck and you can sell them from there."

"Improvisation," purred Einstein. "I like it."

"*That* is against regulation," said Eva sternly.

"Umm, actually it's not," piped up Florence, licking the last crumb of cake from her fingers.

Eva scowled at her.

"Yes, according to the festival rules, the rules that you yourself insisted remained unchanged in order to preserve our heritage, wheeled stalls are permitted," Florence explained. "Because back in the day, a lot of farmers brought goods in on hand carts."

Eva's mouth fell open, then she turned on her heel and stomped off.

"Thanks, Florence," I said.

Tom backed up his truck so it was in line with the other stalls. He flung open the tailgate with a flourish. "Your stall awaits, milady."

"I hope your cakes won't taste of motor oil," commented Einstein.

Sylvia came over with a pretty blue-and-white check tablecloth.

"Here, love, have this," she said. "It'll spruce things up nicely."

"Thank you," I stuttered, overcome by her generosity.

Sylvia nodded her head towards Eva, who was now terrorising a woman selling hand-made soap. "Ignore her," she said. "Her bark is worse than her bite." Then she laughed. "I'm not sure that's true about little Charlie though."

As I draped the cloth over Tom's tailgate, I caught sight of a face I recognised heading my way. Sally Barnes, the woman who had given me a lift to Briarwood Gables when I first arrived, was shepherding a brood of children past. She gave me a warm, if somewhat tired, smile.

"Josie," she said. "How are you settling into your new house?" She nodded at my boxes of goodies. "Looks like you're going to fit right into Briarvale."

"I'm trying," I said.

"We have a stall over the other side of the green," Sally told me. "No money's been released from the house sale yet, so we're counting on selling some jams and pies to tide us over, aren't we, kids?"

My heart ached for her. "Well, you've certainly got your hands full."

Sally rolled her eyes. "This is Todd," she told me, laying a hand on the shoulder of a lanky teenager with stormy eyes.

Todd grunted an acknowledgement.

"Todd, this is Josie, the lady I was telling you about who's moved into Briarwood Gables."

Todd's head jerked up. For a moment he seemed alarmed, then he looked away.

"And this is Millie." Sally pointed to a girl about eight years old with thick, auburn curls pulled into a ponytail, just like her mother's. "And Poppy," a younger girl hiding behind her mother's legs.

"You look about the same age as my grand-daughters," I told her. "They're six."

Poppy nodded shyly.

"And I'm Benji," declared a chubby boy with a splatter of freckles over his nose. "Have you got cakes? I like cake."

"Benji," chided his mother. "Where are your manners?"

"But I *do* like cake," replied Benji.

"He's all right," I laughed. "Would you all like a piece? On the house? It's my grandmother's special recipe loaf cake made with thyme."

"That's very kind," said Sally.

As I moved to get them some slices of cake, Einstein's paw patted my arm. "These are small children," he warned me. "Find them some small pieces."

Sally and her brood went off munching on Tranquillity Thyme Loaf Cake and I set about laying out the rest of the slices on the tailgate of Tom's truck.

Two stalls down, I noticed Terry Grady grappling with a rickety display stand. His face was flushed, his eyebrows furrowed together as he tried to hold the bars and screw them together by himself. Suddenly, the screwdriver slipped and half of the stand collapsed. Terry hurled the part of the stand he was holding to the floor, along with a string of swear words that made Einstein's ears go flat.

"If anyone needs some Tranquillity Loaf, he does," Einstein commented. "Nothing solves anger issues like sugar and witchcraft."

"And it gives me an excuse to talk to him. Maybe I can find out his alibi for the day of Graham Prescott's murder," I said excitedly. "That is a genius idea."

"That's why you called me Einstein," he purred.

"We'll definitely be able to see if my baking makes a difference on someone who is *that* annoyed," I said.

"Oh, the baking will make a difference alright," said Einstein drily. "The question is, will it be the difference you were hoping for?"

I picked up the largest slice of Tranquillity Loaf I could find, plastered on my biggest smile, and headed over to where Terry was trying to untangle the jigsaw of metal poles that was meant to be the stand.

"Hi," I said, holding out the cake. "It looks like you could use a pick-me-up."

Terry let go of the pole he was holding and took a step backwards. "Well... that's... that's right kind of you," he stuttered. He took the loaf cake I offered and ventured a cautious bite. "Mmm. This is really good."

"Thanks." I watched him closely as I said, "I'm Josie. I just moved into Briarwood Gables."

Terry's eyebrows shot up. "Briarwood? You got more than you bargained for with Prescott being murdered there." He took another bite of loaf cake. "Have the police finished there yet?"

Why would he ask that? Was he the killer?

I shook my head. "They were digging up my path yesterday."

Terry stopped mid-chew. "Why?"

"They wouldn't say," I told him.

Terry shrugged and went back to eating cake. Already I thought his shoulders were starting to ease.

"It's quite a job building all these stands," I said. "I bet you got here early."

"Too right. Been here since six."

"You must be used to it, though. You're a builder, aren't you?"

"Yeah. Own my own business."

"That's great." I took a deep breath. "I heard you were quoting on that big job in Trevenna."

OK, that wasn't smooth, but it was the best I could come up with.

Terry swallowed the last of the cake and frowned slightly. "The only job I've been after in Trevenna was Kyle Ingram's barn conversion. And that's really in the early planning stages. Might not even happen when I give him the price."

"Oh," I blustered. "I must have heard wrong."

But inside I was jubilant. If I could find out where Ingram's barn was, I could check Terry's alibi.

"I should get back to finishing this stall," said Terry, brushing crumbs from his hands. "Thanks for the cake, Josie."

I hurried back to Tom's truck. Einstein was smirking at me from the front seat.

"Nicely done," he murmured. "Witchcraft and baking. We'll make a sleuth out of you yet."

Chapter 23

"**L**ADIES AND GENTLEMEN."

I jumped as Eva Henshaw's voice boomed above the general chatter. She was in the centre of a makeshift stage on the edge of the green, Florence on one side, and Percy and Charlie on the other.

"It is my great pleasure to welcome you all to this year's Great Runaway Egg Festival," Eva declared.

The crowd clapped and cheered, but as Eva waited for them to quieten, Florence strode onto the stage and took the microphone from her hand.

"Prepare yourselves for our first event," she said brightly. "A spectacle of canine skill..."

"Florence Bindle!" Eva interrupted. "What do you think you're doing?"

A ripple of laughter ran around the green.

Florence's eyes widened, but she held her ground. "I'm introducing the duck herding display."

"Oh no, you're not!" Eva lunged for the mic. "*I* do the introductions."

Florence neatly sidestepped Eva. "Tom Carver and his faithful companion, Murphy, will now demonstrate..." she shimmied out of reach as Eva made another grab for her "... the ancient art of duck herding."

The audience roared with laughter.

Percy, ever the neat-freak, adjusted his glasses and hurried forward, pulling Charlie with him. "This is most irregular," he muttered to Florence. "Eva, my dear, perhaps we should..."

We never found out what Percy had in mind because, at that moment, his foot got tangled in Charlie's lead. Time stood still as he teetered on the edge of the stage, arms windmilling in his effort to stay upright. Then he simply toppled off, leaving Charlie to jump off the stage and head for the wood carving stall where, no doubt, he wanted to finish his business.

"Charlie! Smoochipoo!" cried Eva, rushing after the dog. "Come here at once!"

Seizing the moment, Florence marched to the front of the stage. "Without further ado," she announced triumphantly, "I give you Tom and Murphy."

The crowd cheered, although I wasn't sure whether it was for Tom or Florence.

"Well, that was entertaining" commented Einstein. "Looks like your Self-Assured Strawberry Muffins pack quite the punch. Perhaps we should market them as 'armed and dangerous'."

Stifling a laugh, I moved to where a crowd had gathered in a circle. In the middle, Tom and Murphy had set up some brightly painted gates and obstacles. Bonnie and Clyde were waddling about, looking decidedly unimpressed by the onlooking crowd.

As Murphy began herding the reluctant birds around the course, I caught sight of DI Holloway. He met my gaze and gave me a curt nod before turning back to watch Tom.

My stomach clenched.

Was he really interested in duck herding? Or was he using the event to further his investigations?

"Josie!" A bright voice interrupted my thoughts. "Nice to see you again."

It was Madeleine, the Briarvale estate agent.

"Terrible business about Graham Prescott," she said. "Let me know if you ever want to sell."

I opened my mouth to reply, but a man caught her arm.

"Madeleine," he said, in a not-so-pleased tone. "About my house..."

Madeleine's face dropped.

"Can we talk about this on Monday?" she said. "Today's my day off." But the man took her arm and steered her away, so I turned back to the arena where, to the delight of the crowd, Murphy was triumphantly shepherding Bonnie and Clyde into the last pen.

Returning to Tom's truck, I passed Terry Grady sitting under the big tree with Poppy and Millie.

Terry looked up with a relaxed smile. "I sorted that stall," he told me. "And now we're making daisy chains, aren't we, girls?"

Wow, that loaf cake really worked.

Poppy held up a long string of flowers. "Look, Josie," she beamed. "Mine's a crown."

"That's beautiful," I said.

Just then, DI Holloway strode past, his suit jacket off and his sleeves rolled up. He was deep in conversation with one of the festival stewards.

Poppy followed him with her eyes. "That's the policeman who kept asking Mummy all those questions about the dead man," she said matter-of-factly.

"Shh, Poppy," hissed Millie. "You're not supposed to talk about that."

Poppy shrugged and stuck her chin out. "Well, he did. And Mummy said she didn't like that Mr Prescott." She fixed me with a knowing look. "Mummy said he was an evil vulture who'd swindled us, and he deserved everything he got."

"Poppy!" Millie gasped.

"But I know Mummy didn't do it," Poppy went on undeterred, "because she was out looking for Todd that night. Mummy was proper worried cos he wasn't answering his phone."

Something told me that Poppy didn't understand how an alibi worked.

"And Nana was worried about Todd, too, because she came to babysit while Mummy went out," said Poppy. "And Nana missed watching *EastEnders* driving to our house."

"Nooo, silly," Millie argued. "Nana was only worried because she nearly ran over that man with the funny hair on the way to our house. She said he was hiding in the bushes and jumped out. Said she didn't see him till the last minute."

My mind was racing.

Sally hadn't seemed happy about her farm sale. If Graham Prescott had swindled her, and she had no alibi…?

But surely not. Sally Barnes couldn't have killed anyone. Could she?

Before I could process this information, Tom appeared, his face flushed with excitement from the dog and duck show.

"You're not going to believe this," he told us. "Florence is on stage belting out karaoke like she's auditioning for *Britain's Got Talent*."

I listened. "That's Florence?" I gasped, trying to see the stage through the crowd.

If I'd doubted magic before this moment, I was now a true believer.

"Florence is good," Terry commented. "Who knew she had it in her?"

Florence ended her song, arms flung wide. Immediately, Eva swooped in and snatched the mic from her hand.

"Thank you, Florence," she trilled. "And now, ladies and gentlemen, please make your way to Briar Hill. The Great Runaway Egg Race is about to begin!"

"Come on, Josie. You have to try this!" Tom urged.

"Oh boy," Einstein drawled. "Nothing says 'welcome to the neighbourhood' like hurling yourself down a hill after an egg. I hope you're wearing sensible shoes."

"All participants in the Egg Race, please make your way to the top of Briar Hill immediately!" Eva repeated.

Tom was waiting, but I shook my head.

"Oh, no. No, no, no. I'm perfectly happy to watch from here, thank you very much."

"Not a chance, city girl," Tom grinned. "You're getting the full Briarvale experience."

"Don't be a spoilsport," Einstein chimed in, his tail swishing with amusement. "Besides, I want to see if you're as good at running down a hill as you are at fixing clocks."

The cheek!

Leaving Murphy and Einstein in the pickup, I set off up the hill after Tom and the other inhabitants of Briarvale with a mixture of excitement and dread.

"You know," Tom began as we trudged up the increasingly steep incline, "this festival has quite the history."

"Oh?" I panted, struggling to keep up. "Do tell... it'll distract me... from the fact that I'm about to make... a complete fool of myself."

Tom chuckled. "It started as an Easter egg hunt for the children. Then one year, a local artist made this massive, ornamental wooden egg. They put it at the top of Briar Hill as a feature for the festival. Heaven knows why they thought that was a good place. Anyway, during the hunt, the egg broke free and rolled down the hill. The whole village ended up chasing after it. It was chaos, but the good kind, you know?"

"And you recreate that chaos every year?" I asked, raising an eyebrow.

"Exactly!" Tom grinned, looking far too excited for a man about to chase eggs down a hill.

Out of breath, I reached the top of the hill. Men were gathered on right hand side, women in the middle, and children on the left where there was a the gentler slope.

From way below us on the village green, Eva's voice rang out. "On your marks."

A group of officials in high-vis jackets were wrestling to open a bag full of large, brightly coloured, wooden eggs.

"Get set!" boomed Eva.

Tom turned to me. "Ready to become a real Briarvale resident?"

"As I'll ever be," I muttered.

"GO!"

The eggs were released, bouncing and wobbling wildly down the hill. And so were we. Villagers surged forward like a tidal wave, all vying for egg-chasing glory. I was instantly overtaken by scores of people, but I found myself laughing. Less than a week ago I was sitting in Crème de la Crumb. Now I was running down a hill like a maniac.

And boy, was I running. My legs were picking up speed of their own accord. I tried to slow down, but my foot slipped on a long tuft of grass and suddenly everything went topsy-turvy.

The world became a blur of grass and sky as I tumbled head over heels towards the village green. I caught glimpses of horrified faces as my fellow egg-chasers jumped out of my way.

Then... thud. I came to an abrupt stop at the bottom of the hill. As I lay there, staring up at the spinning sky, Einstein's face swam into view. He patted my cheek with his paw.

"Oh, good, you're still alive," he drawled. "You know, I've never had to worry about one of my witches trying to kill themselves before."

"You encouraged me!" I retorted.

"And I've learned my lesson," he said. "You need proper training before next year."

"There won't be a next year," I groaned.

"Josie! Are you all right?" Tom's face appeared next to Einstein's.

Shakily, I sat up, checking all my limbs were still attached. "I think so," I stuttered.

Tom offered a hand and pulled me to my feet. "Well, I've got to say," he said, "when you commit to something, you *really* commit. I think you might have beaten the egg down the hill."

"Happy I could entertain." I brushed the grass from my hair, wincing as I discovered a few new bruises. "Did you fare any better?"

"No, he didn't," said Einstein.

Tom shrugged, a sheepish grin on his face. "Let's say neither of us will be crowned Egg Chase Champion this year."

"Thank goodness," Einstein's voice piped up. "I was worried you'd have to wear one of those ridiculous hats."

On the stage, Eva and Florence were in a heated argument about who was to present the winners' prizes, which did appear to include large, brown, egg-shaped hats. I stifled a laugh. Despite the bruises, the grass stains, and my less-than-graceful descent down the hill, I felt more at home than I had in years.

Chapter 24

I LIMPED BACK TOWARDS Tom's truck.

On the stage, Florence was introducing the Briarvale Primary School string ensemble.

"Is that Millie?" I asked, surprised to see Sally's eldest daughter expertly tuning a violin.

Tom nodded. "Little Millie's quite the talent," he said. "And the guy with the baton, that's Harold Whitaker, local librarian turned conductor."

A hush fell over the crowd as the children began to play, and I noticed Sally wiping a tear from her eye.

"Not exactly the London Philharmonic," Einstein muttered, "but they've got heart."

As we stood listening, a tall, lean man with a shock of white, mad-professor hair walked past.

"Doctor Hale!" Tom called. "Good to see you. How's that guttering I fixed last week? I hope it's stopped leaking now."

"It's perfect, Tom. Thank you." Doctor Hale looked at me. "I'm glad to see we didn't need to call an ambulance for you, young lady. That was quite the tumble."

No-one had called me 'young lady' for as long as I could remember. I smiled at him gratefully.

"Yes, I'll have the bruises to remind me tomorrow, but no permanent damage," I said.

"Doc, this is Josie Appleton, the new owner of Briarwood Gables," Tom explained. "Josie, meet Doctor Vincent Hale."

Doctor Hale's keen eyes studied me for a moment. "Ah, Briarwood Gables. Terrible business with Prescott, but if anyone had to die, best it was him."

I blinked, taken aback by his bluntness. "You didn't like Graham?"

Doctor Hale snorted, pushing his glasses up his nose. "That's putting it mildly."

"The doc's an ambassador for healthy eating," Tom explained. "He objected to the new health spa they're building on Sally's farm."

"A health spa sounds very... well, healthy," I said.

Doctor Hale shook his head vigorously. "The company that's running it is all about Botox and liposuction," he explained. "Nothing to do with well-being. Quackery, I call it. But men like Prescott don't care. They just want to line their own pockets."

I felt a chill run down my spine. The doctor was really passionate about the cause. Could dislike of a health spa be motive enough for murder?

Wait a minute! Man with wild hair? Doctor Hale certainly qualified for that description. Millie had told us that her nana had nearly run someone over on the night of the murder. Had the doctor been hiding in the bushes?

I sat on the tailgate of Tom's truck in the April sunshine watching the children competing in the egg and spoon races (introduced by Eva) and then the Easter bonnet competition (with Florence on the mic).

After half an hour, I'd sold all my baking, which almost doubled the money in my purse. Of course, I'd hoped to solve Graham Prescott's murder, but instead I'd gained even more suspects. It was hopeless. Maybe it would have been different if I'd got the honesty cookies right.

Disappointed, I went to the HoneyPot Tearoom and bought coffees and two baguettes filled to bursting with cheese and salad. I gave one to Tom, and we sat on the tailgate watching the festival, with Einstein and Murphy at our feet.

"Thanks for all your help today," I said. "I really appreciated it."

"That's OK," said Tom gruffly. He shifted uncomfortably. "Umm... There's something I've been meaning to ask you, Josie." He stared out over the festival ground, not looking at me. "You see Beatrix, she... she left money to pay me for looking after Briarwood Gables. She said it would last until you came to live here."

My eyebrows shot up. "She did?"

If Beatrix had left money, that could change everything.

Tom's fingers tapped nervously on his cup. "I suppose that means ... well, it's up to you now whether I continue to live and work there."

"Oh," I managed, eloquently.

"Don't worry if you want me out. I'll be fine," he hurried on. He jumped off the tailgate. "I should go and fetch the crate with the ducks in."

I slumped against the side of the truck as he disappeared into the crowd. "Einstein," I groaned, "what am I supposed to do now?"

The cat stretched lazily. "Ah, yes. Do you get rid of the ruggedly handsome handyman? Quite the conundrum."

"That's not helping," I muttered.

"Well," Einstein drawled, "if you're asking for my feline wisdom, I'd say, your grandmother was many things, but a fool wasn't one of them. She had excellent taste in familiars, after all."

I snorted. "You're so modest."

"My point is," Einstein continued, "Beatrix was an excellent judge of character. Perhaps you should consider that before making any hasty decisions about Tom."

After that, I went into Fletcher's Fine Goods Store and filled the boxes that I'd brought the baking in full of groceries. I was heading for the till when Eva swept in with Charlie trotting at her heels like a small, yappy satellite. Ignoring the fact I clearly was there first, she barged in front of me to the counter.

"Hello, Edwin," she trilled. "Charlie's hoping you have some of his favourite doggy treats in stock, aren't you, Mummy's little darling?"

"I do," said Edwin, his voice a touch stiff. "I've put them to one side especially for him."

"Ooh, do you hear that, Charliekins," cooed Eva. "That nice Mr Fletcher's got them just for you."

Charlie started running in delirious little circles as Edwin placed two bags of treats on the counter.

"Well, I'm glad you've got them back in stock," said Eva. "It was most inconvenient having to drive to Polvarren to buy them. I don't know why you couldn't get them before."

Edwin didn't meet her gaze. "Supply chain issues," he said quickly, opening the till. "But everything's good now."

Eva huffed slightly as she took the treats off the counter. "And don't forget the extra town council planning meeting tomorrow," she reminded him. "We have the Silverbrook Mine plan to consider, and we still have lots of issues to thrash out with this health spa. I know you're a big supporter, but..."

"Oh, I won't be backing it now that Prescott's dead," Edwin interrupted.

Eva took a step backwards. "Oh," she said, clearly surprised. "That's quite a turn-around."

Edwin pulled at his collar. "Well, I've had time to think and the whole thing's a mess," he muttered. "All that extra traffic jamming up our country lanes. Downright dangerous, if you ask me. Not what the village needs."

"But Edwin," said Eva slowly, "that is what we've all been saying for months. You were the one pushing it through. Honestly, if it hadn't been for you..."

"Well, things change," Edwin cut in, his tone sharp. "I don't have to explain myself."

"Right. Well. Fine." Eva grabbed Charlie's treats and huffed out the door, muttering to herself.

Edwin let out a breath and ran a hand over his bald patch. "Eva thinks she knows everything," he grumbled.

Finally, he seemed to notice I was still standing there, arms full of grocery boxes.

"Oh, sorry, Josie," he said briskly, straightening up and reaching for the till. "Let's sort you out."

I set the boxes down and watched him ring my shopping through.

Were his hands moving a bit too fast? His smile a bit too bright? Was he overcompensating? Trying to look like someone who *hadn't* murdered Graham Prescott?

I took my change, thanked him, and turned to leave.

I didn't know Edwin Fletcher, but the more I saw of him...the guiltier he looked.

Chapter 25

I CARRIED MY GROCERIES back to the pickup. Tom was securing the crate with Bonnie and Clyde in the back.

"Of course, you must stay at Briarwood," I told him. "But I'm not sure I'll be able to pay you. I don't have an income right now. I'll have to ask the solicitor about any money my grandmother left."

Tom let out a sigh of relief. "That's OK," he said. "Maybe I could pay you rent for staying in the caravan."

"Don't be silly," I said, waving the idea away. "But I was thinking I could turn Briarwood into a Bed and Breakfast."

Tom's eyebrows shot up. "That'd be a good idea," he said. "And if you need any help, you only have to ask."

I stowed my groceries in the front of the truck.

"Well, well," purred Einstein. "Who'd have thought you'd fit right in with these country bumpkins. Are you serious about the B&B idea?"

I nodded, suddenly worried about how Einstein would take the news. He sat curled on the seat, his tail flicking from side to side.

"It's a good plan," he said. "You're not the first witch to have guests staying at Briarwood."

I let out a long breath.

But Tom was still watching me. His brows drawn together like he was trying to work something out. "I hope you don't mind me asking," he said hesitantly. "I mean, tell me to mind my own business, but…"

I watched as a red blush crept up his neck. Oh dear, what other bombshells did he have?

"Well, I wondered…" Tom pointed to the ring on my wedding finger. "Are you married?"

I bit my lip. "Technically, yes," I admitted. "But Gary left me."

Tom's eyes grew wide. "Oh," he said, like he wasn't sure whether he should say something comforting or keep quiet. In the end, curiosity won out. "Left, as in…"

"As in didn't say goodbye and vanished." I bit my lip. "Last I heard, he might be in Paraguay."

"Paraguay!" Tom stared at me in disbelief. "Wow. That's not just leaving. That's full-on abandon ship. What a… what an idiot."

"I thought that too," I agreed with a wry smile. "He left me with a mountain of debt and no home on my birthday, five days ago."

"What?" he spluttered, eyes blazing. "Five days ago? And it was your birthday?"

I forced a small shrug. "Yup. I'd hoped to go out for a meal and watch a band. Instead, I got a financial disaster, a missing husband, and a half-melted cake."

"Wow, that's low." Tom's jaw clenched, and for a moment he seemed to be debating whether he wanted to punch something… or someone. "He didn't deserve you," he muttered. "Not even close."

"Yeah, well," I twisted the ring round my finger. "Things hadn't been good between us for a while."

Tom hesitated. "Then you came here?"

I nodded. "But I didn't know anything about the inheritance until my birthday," I explained.

Tom looked at me thoughtfully. "So, that's why you didn't arrive straight away after Beatrix passed?"

"My mother died when I was a baby and my father wouldn't have anything to do with her side of the family," I explained. "Also, my grandmother had left strict instructions for the deeds not to be delivered until my fiftieth birthday."

Tom shook his head. "Why did she do that?"

I shrugged. I wasn't about to mention the magical inheritance that came into being when I hit that milestone. He wouldn't believe that. I barely believed it myself.

The light was fading now, and strings of fairy lights flickered to life around the green, bathing everything in a soft, magical glow.

"Hey, there's a band onstage tonight," Tom said. "We should stay. You didn't get to go out properly on your birthday. This could be a belated celebration. They do line dancing. It's a laugh."

I hesitated.

Even though Gary had left me in debt and chaos, I was still married. And then there was Graham Prescott, murdered mere metres from my house. Should I really be thinking about dancing?

But what the heck? It was line dancing, not a candlelit waltz. And *I* hadn't killed anyone. Surely, I was allowed a night where I didn't feel my world was spinning out of control.

"Yes," I decided. "I'd like that. And hey, I've got a question for you," I said, glancing over at Tom. "Do you know much about Edwin Fletcher?"

Tom frowned at the question, but at the same time he looked relieved, like he'd been bracing himself for something more personal.

"Edwin? He's run the Briarvale store since before most of us were born," he said. "What do you want to know?"

I hesitated. Suggesting old Edwin might have murdered Graham Prescott suddenly seemed silly based on a few odd comments and a sudden burst of cheerful singing. But Tom was waiting. "It's... I've been thinking about the murder, and when I was in the store Edwin said he wouldn't be backing the health spa project now Graham's dead. And the other day Sylvia told me she'd noticed Edwin had been unusually cheerful recently. Singing, even."

Tom looked at me. "Josie Appleton, are you trying to solve the murder?" he said with a grin.

"He's got you," Einstein commented.

I shifted in my seat, suddenly very interested in a crumb on my jumper. "Well, the quicker the killer's caught, the sooner DI Holloway stops sniffing around."

Tom nodded. "Umm, you noticed Holloway too, eh?" He scratched his head. "Well, Edwin was a big supporter of the spa. He used to mention it every time you were in the shop." Suddenly, his eyes opened wide. "And, now you come to mention it, there was this one day I was in at the same time as Prescott. Edwin looked really jumpy, and Prescott said something like, 'You know what'll happen if they vote against me.' He said it quietly, you know, but I heard it. Gave me the creeps."

I sat up straighter. "I know Edwin's on the planning committee," I reasoned. "Looks like Graham was threatening Edwin to make him help him."

"It's possible," said Tom. "But Edwin can be a funny old stick. If people do things to upset him, their favourite biscuits mysteriously vanish from the shelves."

"Like the treats for Eva's dog," I gasped.

"I suppose," said Tom.

He looked confused, but now it was all making sense.

"That gives Edwin motive," I said. "And he might be old, but Edwin still lugs all the boxes around in the shop. I'm sure he'd be capable of giving Prescott a good clout with a candlestick, if he wanted to."

Tom laughed.

"But what about opportunity?" I wondered. "Where was Edwin when Prescott was killed?"

"Tricky one," Tom agreed. "I haven't a clue."

We sat quietly for a moment, then Tom gave me a lop-sided smile.

"So, who else is on your suspect list, Miss Marple? Hope it isn't me?"

Einstein gave a satisfied flick of his tail. "Now we might be getting somewhere."

We sat in the truck waiting for the evening entertainment to start and I told Tom about my suspicions about Terry Grady, Doctor Hale, and even Sally Barnes.

"I don't believe it's Sally," said Tom.

Chapter 26

A T THAT MOMENT, ALMOST as if they knew we'd been talking about their family, Todd wandered past shepherding the younger kids in front of him. They made a beeline for Murphy, who had flopped down beside the stage, soaking up attention like a local celebrity.

Poppy threw her arms around his neck. "He's so soft," she said dreamily, resting her cheek on his fur.

Millie began weaving daisies into his collar, while little Benji tried to get him to shake paws.

Sally appeared moments later, cheeks flushed and a satisfied smile on her face. "You lot are still going strong," she said. She ruffled Todd's hair. "You've done a brilliant job looking after the others today, sweetheart. Honestly, I don't know what I'd have done without you."

Todd gave a nonchalant shrug, but his ears turned pink.

"And I sold every last jar of jam," Sally grinned. "Even the bramble and beetroot one. I've got enough cash to tide us over a couple of weeks at least."

"Does that mean we can have an ice-cream?" Benji asked. "I like ice-cream."

Sally nodded.

"Yay!" the younger kids shouted in unison, and they dashed off towards the ice-cream van with Sally chasing after them.

Todd was less enthusiastic. Tom nodded at him. "You've got a real way with that dog."

"Yeah, he's cool," Todd said, scratching Murphy's ears.

"If you ever want to come up to Briarwood Gables," I offered, "you're welcome. Tom's got chickens, ducks, and a goose who likes to steal things. You'd be more than welcome to hang out with them."

To my surprise, Todd stepped back like I'd suggested he scrub floors for a week.

"Uh... no thanks," he said quickly. "I'm... I'm good."

Then he mumbled something about ice-cream and walked off, hands stuffed in his pockets, eyes on the ground.

I watched him go, puzzled. "You never can tell with teenagers," I said.

Tom sighed. "Todd is Sally's boy from her first marriage. His dad left before he was born, and now his stepdad's died in that accident. It's a lot for a kid to deal with."

"Poor Todd," I murmured, watching him disappear into the crowd. "I can't help feeling like he needs someone in his corner."

We were silent for a moment, then Tom said, "I don't know if you know this, but my wife died. She had cancer."

"Oh, I'm so sorry," I said.

Tom nodded. "It was nearly twenty years ago now. And I was going through some pretty rough times. Your grandmother fought in my corner. And I see you have inherited her good nature."

"That's not all she inherited," commented Einstein, with a flick of his tail.

Before we could say anything else, Eva's voice boomed from the speakers. "Ladies and gentlemen, the moment you've all been waiting for! Please welcome our fabulous band, The Haystack Howlers!"

The band launched into a twanging intro, just as Florence leapt onto the stage beside Eva, still clearly riding high on self-assurance muffins. There was a brief tug-of-war before Florence seized the microphone and hollered, "Let's rock, Briarvale!" Then she twirled across the stage with surprising agility, dragging the bemused lead singer of the band into a dance which looked something like a startled chicken navigating a minefield.

"Well, you heard the lady," said Tom, offering me his hand with a crooked smile. "Time to prove your Briarvale spirit."

I laughed. "If I fall over again, I'm blaming you."

We joined the others forming rows in front of the stage. Florence was already shouting steps. Her instructions didn't seem to have anything to do with the dance, but it didn't matter. We stomped, clapped, and turned, laughing with the rest of the crowd. Even Eva joined in eventually, although she kept trying to correct Florence's choreography mid-song.

All too soon, the band played one final flourish. A cheer went up that echoed round the village. Eva grabbed the microphone again, but Florence had already dived in front of her.

"Thank you, Briarvale! That concludes the Great Runaway Egg Festival!" she shouted triumphantly.

"No, I conclude it," Eva barked, jabbing the mic button.

The two of them tussled for control of the announcement while the crowd roared with laughter. The fairy lights glowed above us, making everything magic. It was chaotic, messy, and weirdly perfect.

And then I spotted DI Holloway watching from the edge of the crowd.

The laughter around me dimmed a little.

Because no matter how good the music was, the murder hadn't gone away.

The drive back to Briarwood Gables was a blur of twinkling stars and shadowy hedgerows. Tom's pickup rumbled along the winding country lanes, the fading echoes of the festival still ringing in my ears.

"You're very quiet," said Tom as we pulled up the drive to the house.

I took a breath. "It's... it's been such a perfect day, and I'm sad it's ended," I admitted, surprising myself with my honesty. "For the first time in a long while, I felt like I belonged, you know?"

The light of the dashboard lit up Tom's smile. "Well, that's because you *do* belong, Josie," he told me. "And don't worry, there'll be plenty more nights like this. Briarvale's big on festivals. Any excuse for cake, dancing and chaos."

I smiled, but my eyes drifted to the greenhouse as we pulled up outside the house. It was in darkness now. The police tape still fluttered round the vegetable patch, but I couldn't see any officers lurking near the glass. It looked like they'd finally left us alone.

Tom helped me carry my boxes of groceries into the kitchen, then with a tired wave, he and Murphy disappeared towards the caravan with Bonnie and Clyde waddling after them. I trudged up the stairs, every muscle reminding me of the dancing, the hill climb, and my not-so-graceful descent. Who knew that being a novice witch and amateur sleuth could be so tiring?

But even as I crawled into bed, my thoughts wouldn't settle. They twisted and tangled, looping back over the murder and the odd fragments of conversation I'd collected like puzzle pieces that didn't quite fit.

Edwin Fletcher, possibly being blackmailed by Prescott?

Terry Grady, business ruined by Prescott's false promises.

Dr Hale, furious about the spa threatening his patients.

Even Sally, who'd been out looking for Todd the night Graham died, felt she'd been swindled by Prescott in the farm sale.

Everyone in Briarvale had secrets, and somehow, I'd landed right in the middle of them.

I closed my eyes, but sleep didn't come easily.

There was an owl hooting somewhere close. The wind was rustling the ivy on the windowsill. Even the warmth of Einstein sitting on my feet didn't calm me down.

What had Graham Prescott been doing near my greenhouse?

Why were the police lifting my flagstones?

And I thought Gary leaving his family had been the most unexpected thing in my life.

Family?

With a jolt, I realised I'd not called Kim back after my baking emergency. I pulled out my phone. Sure enough there were five calls I'd missed while I was dancing.

Hastily, I wrote her a text message.

Had a great day at the Easter Festival. Will tell you all about it soon. Love, Mum xxx

Tomorrow, I promised myself, I'd tell her everything that had happened.

Chapter 27

S UNLIGHT STREAMED THROUGH THE chintz curtains. It was
another glorious day, by the look of it.

Then I rolled over to check the time.

Every part of my body screamed in protest. I had bruises from
tumbling down the hill, aching legs from dancing, and feet that felt
like they'd gone a few rounds with a steamroller. I abandoned checking
the time and flopped back with a groan.

"You really will need to get in training if you're going to survive in
Briarvale," said a voice from the end of the bed.

"Shut up, Einstein," I yawned.

"Well, I'm tired too," Einstein grumbled. "I've not been to a festival
in years."

Eventually, I rolled out of bed and shuffled to the window. The sky
was a perfect spring blue, the hedgerows sparkled with dew, and tiny
white lambs frisked on the rolling hills beyond. I opened the window,
breathing in the morning air.

If I leaned out of the window far enough, I could just see the
greenhouse. It was empty. The police had definitely gone.

Humming to myself, I pulled the old blue cardigan I'd brought from London over my pyjamas and limped down the stairs to make breakfast.

"Someone's in a good mood," Einstein purred from his perch on the windowsill. "Did Tom's dancing sweep you off your feet?"

I stirred my porridge, feeling a blush creep up my cheeks. "I'm just happy to be here. Yesterday's festival was wonderful, and yes, Tom is... nice."

Einstein's whiskers twitched with amusement. "Nice? Is that what they're calling it these days?"

I decided ignoring him was the best policy. "Anyway," I told him breezily, "today I'm going to start on the house. It's time to pull off all the dust sheets and figure out what it'll take to get my B&B running."

Einstein eyed my porridge critically. "You're going to have to do better than that if you're going to impress paying guests," he commented.

I was about to retort when movement outside the window caught my eye. DI Holloway was striding along the path towards the trees where Tom's caravan was parked. He was followed by three uniformed officers.

My heart skipped a beat.

"That can't be good," Einstein muttered, echoing my thoughts.

Abandoning my breakfast, I pushed my feet into the pair of oversized wellies by the door and hurried after them.

Einstein and I arrived at the caravan in time to hear DI Holloway pounding on the door. Seconds later, Tom emerged from the direction of the river, barefoot and holding a towel.

(I really must tell him it's fine for him to use the shower in the house.)

"Mr Carver," said the DI, stepping forward to meet him. "You are under arrest on suspicion of the murder of Graham Prescott. You have the right to remain silent…"

"What?" I gasped.

Tom stopped, water still dripping from his hair. "I've already told you everything I know," he stuttered.

"Nevertheless," Holloway said, nodding to two of the officers. "Take him in."

Einstein flicked his tail. "Actually, this is *really* bad."

"Hey! Wait! This is a mistake." My feet slid around inside the huge wellingtons, which flopped awkwardly with every step as I staggered across the wet grass, hurrying as fast as I could, my aching legs forgotten.

As the officers led Tom towards the waiting cars, he caught my eye. "Josie," he said, his voice strained. "Look after the animals… and figure this out, eh?"

I nodded. "I will," I promised.

Murphy set off after Tom, but he reluctantly came to stand with me when I called his name.

I could see it was no use arguing with the officers. They were simply following orders. I needed someone higher up. I turned in time to see DI Holloway disappearing inside the caravan after the remaining officer.

"Excuse me!" I called, storming inside after them. "What in the name of Earl Grey do you think you are doing?"

DI Holloway was rifling through the cupboard by Tom's bed, his hands covered in plastic gloves, while the other officer was pulling tins out of the cupboard over the oven.

Holloway arched an eyebrow at the sight of me in my stripy pyjamas and six-sizes-too-big wellingtons.

"Mrs Appleton," he said, barely hiding a grin. "How well do you know Mr Carver?"

Einstein hopped onto the doorstep and Murphy pushed beside me, a low growl rumbling in his throat.

"I know Tom well enough to know you've arrested the wrong man," I retorted, crossing my arms and wishing that I'd at least dragged a brush through my hair before challenging the law.

"Mr Carver's fingerprints were found on the murder weapon," said DI Holloway flatly.

"The candlestick? Of course his fingerprints were on it. He's been using it to prop the greenhouse door open for years!"

Holloway's expression didn't alter. "A bit convenient, don't you think?"

"For holding the door? Yes," I shot back.

Holloway didn't react. "And we found something buried under a flagstone along your path," he went on. "Know anything about that?"

"Why would I?" I bristled. "What was it?"

"I'm not at liberty to disclose that information," he said. "But Graham Prescott's phone records show he called Mr Carver shortly before he was murdered."

I looked at him. Was he an idiot?

"Well, that just proves Tom's innocent," I said. "Graham Prescott called him to offer him that fake job. He must have wanted him out of the way."

Holloway's expression didn't change. "And why would he do that?"

I threw up my hands. "I don't know," I said. "You're supposed to be the detective."

Holloway turned away and started rifling through Tom's waste bin. "Did you know Mr Carver has a police record?" he said, without looking up. "Vandalism. Twenty years ago."

"Twenty years ago?" I fumed. "Goodness, that's practically a character reference. It's probably before you were even born?"

DI Holloway's eyes narrowed, and he opened his mouth to speak but then thought better of it. Instead, he pounced on something in the bin, pulling it out with a triumphant flourish.

"Aha," he said.

The other officer gave a knowing nod.

Holloway held up a business card, torn in half.

I didn't need to see the whole thing. Even from the doorway, I could see the name 'Graham Prescott' printed on it. It was the card he'd given me that first morning. The one I'd ripped up and thrown there.

"Oh bother," groaned Einstein.

The DI gave me a smug grin, placed the card in a plastic bag as though he'd recovered the Crown Jewels, and sealed the bag shut. "Seems Mr Carver not only knew the victim, but he was angry enough to rip this up."

Murphy gave a sharp bark, and I placed my hand on his back.

"Well, you've got that wrong, too," I blustered. "That's the card that Graham gave *me* when he called the morning I arrived. *I* ripped it up and threw it in Tom's bin."

Even before I'd finished speaking, I realised that wasn't the smartest thing to admit.

"Really?" The DI looked at me for a long moment. "In our first interview, you told me you'd only just met Mr Carver, and yet you seem very friendly. Now you've admitted to being in his caravan. You were dancing together at the festival yesterday. You..."

"I don't like what you are insinuating," I interrupted. My face burned so hot I was surprised I didn't spontaneously combust, but I met his gaze unflinchingly. "We weren't dancing *to-geth-er*," I said, splitting the words up like I was explaining to a three-year-old. "We were line dancing... in a line... with everyone else."

DI Holloway gave a weary shake of his head. "Look, I'm just doing my job, Mrs Appleton," he said. "Following procedures."

"Procedures, my backside," I muttered under my breath.

"Carry on here," Holloway said to the other officer, pulling his car keys out of his pocket. "And check Carver's vehicle before you leave."

I stepped to one side to allow Holloway to exit the caravan. The sooner he was gone, the better.

As he passed me, he gave me a long, pointed look. "Don't leave town, Mrs Appleton."

I glowered at him, resisting the urge to give him a sarcastic salute.

Where was Mr Tuppyhead? I looked round the caravan, praying the goat would appear to give Holloway a proper Briarwood Gables send off. Disappointingly, the goat was nowhere to be seen.

Instead, Agatha was pecking the ground near the hen coop. As the DI passed her, his car keys jingled. And that was all it took.

Agatha's head jerked up, and with speed worthy of a feathery ninja, she lunged for the keys in his hand, snapping at the air just millimetres from his fingers.

"Good grief!" Holloway jumped back, shaking the evidence bag in Agatha's face.

"She likes shiny things," I said sweetly, trying not to laugh. "You might want to hold those a little higher."

DI Holloway picked up the pace as he headed for his car, but Agatha was relentless. Wings half-spread, she waddled after him at an impressive speed, aiming well-targeted pecks at the keyring.

Holloway let out a very undetective-like yelp and broke into an awkward jog, Agatha honking triumphantly in pursuit.

I leaned against the caravan and watched as he scrambled into his car with the speed of a man fleeing his own crime scene. Agatha gave his tyres a last irritated peck before fluffing her feathers and strutting off.

"Good work, Agatha," I murmured.

Einstein jumped off the caravan step, his tail swishing from side to side. "So, what's your plan now?"

I looked at him, then at Murphy, whose tail had drooped. "Now," I said, straightening up, "it's time to solve this case."

Chapter 28

THE SMELL OF BURNING porridge wafted from the kitchen, a bitter reminder of how quickly my earlier happiness had gone up in smoke. My mind whirled with questions, but one thing was clear: I needed answers, and I needed them now.

"Are we making honesty cookies again?" Einstein asked, as I shook off the wellington boots.

"No time for that," I told him. "And there's no guarantee they'd work anyway."

I dumped what was left of the porridge in the bin.

"No. But I've watched enough episodes of *Murder She Wrote* to know when it's time for some good old-fashioned sleuthing."

I marched upstairs.

"So, what's first?" Einstein asked, neatly dodging the clean jumper I flung out of the wardrobe.

"I still favour Terry Grady as a suspect," I said, hastily splashing water on my face. "He mentioned the job he quoted for was a barn conversion at somewhere called Ingram's farm. Do you know where that is?"

"No," said Einstein. "It's not somewhere I ever went with your grandmother."

"OK. We go into the village and ask Sylvia," I decided, pulling the jumper over my head. "She'll know."

The last police car was disappearing out of my drive as I set off to walk into Briarvale.

Pity, I could have used the lift. But at least they must have finished with the caravan and Tom's pickup.

The pickup!

Would he mind if I drove it?

It would be much quicker than walking, especially with my aching muscles. And it was for his benefit, after all.

There had to be keys.

Was Tom the sort who left them on the sun visor?

No.

I raced to the caravan. Houdini, the sheep, was blocking the doorway, staring at me like he was daring me to pass.

I hesitated.

Now was not the time for being intimidated by farm animals.

"Shoo!" I gave Houdini's woolly head a gentle push, and thankfully he sidled off, the bell round his neck jangling cheerily.

"Keys. Keys," I muttered, scanning round the van. Holloway and the other officer had left things strewn everywhere.

"Hanging over the door," purred Einstein, appearing beside me.

"Nice work, Watson."

I grabbed the keyring and headed to the truck.

Murphy jumped on the seat the second I opened the door.

"You're not bringing the mutt, are you?" Einstein grumbled, hopping delicately onto the dashboard out of the way of Murphy's bushy, wagging tail.

Murphy looked at me expectantly with his big brown, puppy-dog eyes.

"Yes, Murphy's coming," I said, fiddling to get the key in the ignition.

"Bah," said Einstein, curling his tail round his body indignantly.

The engine roared into life on the first try.

Good start.

But Tom was a lot taller than me. The seat was set for someone with legs like a giraffe. I fiddled around, looking for the adjustment lever.

When I found it, it was stuck.

Not so good.

In the end, I stuffed one of Tom's coats behind my back so I could reach the pedals. It wasn't great, but it would have to do.

I jammed the pickup into what I hoped was first gear. The gearbox was so vague I could have been engaging warp speed for all I knew. I lifted the clutch with a lurch. And we were off.

Driving the pickup was nothing like my executive Range Rover back in London. Its steering was sloppy, its brakes were slow, and every gear change felt like a suggestion rather than a command, but I made it to the village, crawling across the bridge for fear of hitting the stone sides.

I pulled alongside the kerb near the HoneyPot with a sigh of relief.

So far, so good.

And I was sure that Sylvia would be able to shed light on the whereabouts of Ingram's barn.

Around the green, a small army of volunteers were taking down the stalls and the stage from yesterday's festival. The scene rather matched my mood.

I was about to lock the pickup when a voice called, "You should leave a window open."

Todd, Sally's eldest, was leaning against a lamp-post, his arms folded, his scowl back in place.

I really need to make more tranquillity loaf.

He jerked his chin towards the pickup. "For Murphy," he explained. "Dogs can overheat in cars."

"Of course," I said, embarrassed I'd not thought of that. "Thanks for looking out for him."

Todd shrugged and went back to watching the activity on the green.

I was about to lock the pickup a second time, when I had an idea. "Umm. Todd. Would you mind taking Murphy for a walk? Up Briar Hill maybe? I'm sure he'd like that better than sitting in the truck. I'll only be a few minutes. In the tearoom. You'd be doing me a big favour."

Todd lifted a surprised eyebrow. "Yeah, OK, Mrs Appleton," he said. For a moment he forgot himself and I saw a flicker of enthusiasm, before he dialled it back to his usual scowl.

I was about to go into the HoneyPot when Edwin Fletcher caught my arm. I jumped. Edwin was one of my top suspects. I didn't want to be in contact with a potential killer.

"I heard about Tom's arrest," Edwin said.

"Wow, news travels fast in these parts," I said.

Edwin nodded. "If there's anything I can do," he said kindly.

Was it too kindly?

I bit back the urge to ask him to confess he was the real murderer. That would be the most helpful.

At that moment, Sally's Land Rover screeched to a halt beside us.

"Have you seen Todd?" she shouted through the open window, her face pale with worry "The school rang. He never showed up."

Before I could say anything, Edwin stepped up to the window.

"Stay calm, Sally, love," he said reassuringly. "He'll be OK. Tell you what, give me a moment to lock the shop and I'll come and help you look."

His voice was warm and caring. Nothing like a potential killer.

"Oh, Edwin, that's so kind of you, but I couldn't ask you to tramp all over Briarvale again," said Sally, but it didn't sound like it would take much for him to convince her otherwise.

I raised my hand sheepishly, feeling like a schoolgirl confessing to breaking a window. "Umm... actually... I've just seen Todd. He's taken Murphy for a walk up Briar Hill. He's really took a shine to that dog."

Sally looked towards the hillside. Sure enough, there was Todd throwing a stick with Murphy bounding after it. She let out a long breath, her shoulders sagging with relief.

"There you go," said Edwin. "Mystery solved." He gave us both a smile. "I'd best get back to work."

"I swear, that boy will be the death of me," she said, pulling her hair into a ponytail.

"I'm sorry. I didn't realise he should be in school," I said.

Sally climbed out of the Land Rover and shut the door. "Todd's been really off these last few days," Sally told me. "Moody. Quiet. Then yesterday, at the festival, I thought we'd turned a corner. He seemed so relaxed. He was good with the little ones. And now..." She shot a glance in the direction of Briar Hill, "Now, he's bunking off school again." Her eyes were shiny with tears.

I nodded sympathetically.

"Todd has no father figure," Sally continued, her words tumbling out like water from a broken dam. "I'm at my wit's end, Josie. I don't know what to do anymore."

"Look, I was going into the HoneyPot," I told her. "Why not let Todd have a bit of fun with Murphy, and I'll buy you a coffee while we wait for them to come back? You look like you could use a drink."

The bell above the HoneyPot's door jingled merrily and the comforting smell of coffee, frying bacon, and cinnamon rolls enveloped us. The tearoom was quiet, just two men in the corner tucking into egg on toast.

Einstein settled himself on the windowsill by my usual table and proceeded to mew gently.

"Josie, love!" Sylvia's warm voice carried across the room. Already she was reaching for the coffee pot.

Einstein mewed louder until Sylvia said, "And cream for His Lordship."

The mewing changed to a deep, satisfied purr.

"I heard about Tom," said Sylvia, handing me a saucer for Einstein. "What are the police thinking?"

"What's happened to Tom?" Sally asked. The Briarvale grapevine had obviously not reached her yet.

I gulped. "He's been arrested," I said quietly. "For murder."

"No!" Sally clutched at the edge of the counter. "That's... that's ridiculous."

"I know," I said firmly. "Which is why I'm going to find the real killer."

"You are?" asked Sally. "How?"

"Good point," said Einstein, licking up the last drop of cream and settling down to wash his whiskers.

"Well, I'm starting by asking lots of questions." I said. "I mean, I know you were out that night looking for Todd. Did you see anyone acting suspiciously? Anyone you didn't know?"

I watched her closely. I couldn't believe Sally was the murderer, but if she was, asking about that night might prompt a reaction from her.

But Sally simply frowned, thinking hard. "I don't think so," she said. "But you should ask Edwin; he was with me. He might have noticed something."

"Edwin?" I chewed my bottom lip. "Were you and Edwin together?"

"Yeah. I called in the shop first. His grandson's in Todd's class, and I thought he might have heard from Todd. When we realised he hadn't, Edwin came out to help me."

I managed a small smile even as I considered the implications. If Sally and Edwin were together the whole time, unless they were *both* in on the murder, that cleared them.

Which was good news for them, but bad news for Tom.

Chapter 29

THE DOORBELL JINGLED AGAIN and a portly woman wearing an oversized cardigan shuffled in.

"Morning, Annie," called Sylvia. "The usual toasted teacake, is it?"

Annie inched as close to the counter as she could get and lowered her voice. "Not today, Sylv. I'll have one of those fruity teas... and some gluten free toast."

"Ooh, going for the healthy option, are you?" said Sylvia, reaching for the toaster. "Nice."

"Yes, well, Doctor Hale says I have to manage my blood sugar," Annie said solemnly. "Brought me his whole healthy eating plan. Printed it and everything. Came round in person, too, which was very kind of him." She paused and then added, "Although he did arrive right in the middle of the antiques programme on the telly. I missed the ending completely. But anyway, I promised him I'd do this eating thing for a month to see how it goes." She looked longingly at the cinnamon rolls in the cabinet. "Today is the fourth day," she said with a sigh. "And it's not getting any easier."

Sylvia leaned in, too. "What if I made cinnamon toast?" she suggested. "Just a hint of sweetness, and I heard that cinnamon's good for you."

Annie's face brightened. "Oh, Sylvia, you're a dear. That would be lovely." She lowered her voice again. "Don't tell anyone else about... the diet. You know how judgemental some can be about these new-fangled ideas. I told Doctor Hale, 'I appreciate you delivering vegetable boxes, but you keep it a secret'. He promised he would."

I looked at Sally. "Really?" I whispered. "All this cloak-and-dagger business over... eating vegetables."

"In Briarvale, changing your diet is practically an act of revolution," Sally told me with a grin.

Einstein chuckled. "Oh yes. Quinoa smuggling is big business in these parts," he quipped.

They were right. These people could make an issue over the village clock chiming. They made the curtain twitchers back in London look like they'd pulled the blinds and taken up knitting.

"Hey, Josie," Sylvia called. "Have you met Annie? She's one of your neighbours. Lives in the bungalow past the bridge."

I smiled, but I was only half-listening.

Doctor Hale had taken the healthy eating plan round to Annie four days ago! The day of the murder.

I turned to Sally, my mind racing. "What time is the antiques programme on?"

She didn't know, but an internet search gave us the answer. It started at three o'clock and finished at half past. That meant Doctor Hale was at Annie's house at the time someone hit Graham Prescott with the candlestick.

I sighed.

That was another name off my suspect list, which only left Terry Grady.

"And he was the one making daisy chains," commented Einstein. "Never trust a man who's too good with flower crowns."

Todd appeared outside the window with Murphy. His shoulders slumped when he saw his mother sitting at my table.

Sally drained the last of her coffee and gave me a resigned look. "Wish me luck," she said.

I paid Sylvia, noticing with concern how rapidly my money was going down.

But I couldn't worry about that now.

I followed Sally outside.

"Thanks for walking Murphy," I said to Todd, but he barely acknowledged me.

I opened the door of Tom's pickup and Murphy jumped in.

Sally ruffled Todd's hair. "Right," she said. "You and me need to talk."

"Well, that's going to be a fun chat," said Einstein, settling himself on the dashboard as far from Murphy as he could. "And can't you move this dog away from me? He's panting all over me with doggy breath."

There was no way I was going to shift Murphy, but I got him to lie on the seat, then I started the pickup.

"Do you know the way to Trevenna?" Einstein asked.

"No," I admitted. "But there's a signpost at the crossroads."

Einstein sighed. "Turn right," he said. "And watch for the tight bend."

With Einstein barking directions like a snarky, furry satnav, I eased Tom's pickup out along the main street and headed south, out of Briarvale.

The sun flickered through the trees as we rumbled along the narrow, hedge-lined roads. Birds darted from branch to branch, and a tractor chugged somewhere nearby.

I rounded a bend, and the tractor appeared. Enormous tyres. Slow as molasses. Coming straight at us. I slammed on the brakes, and the pickup slowed to a halt.

"Umm, Einstein. Bit of a tight squeeze," I gasped.

"Gateway on the left," he said, as cool as anything.

I squeezed as close to the gate as I dared (which Einstein told me wasn't very close at all), and the tractor trundled past with a regal wave of the driver's hand.

Back on the road, I followed Einstein's directions until we passed a man in a waxed jacket walking a spaniel.

I slowed and wound down the window. "Excuse me! I'm looking for Ingram's farm?"

He gave me a curious look, taking in the pickup, the unfamiliar face, and possibly the cat on the dashboard.

"Up the hill, turn right at the sign for Trevenna, then it's the third gate on your left. Long drive. Big brick barn you can't miss."

"Thanks!" I called, and drove on, the tyres crunching over gravel as we found the gate in question.

"How exactly are you going to go about this?" asked Einstein, sighing with annoyance as he slid across the dashboard as we bounced over the potholes on the drive.

"I have an idea," I said.

We rumbled into the farmyard and I pulled up near the sheep pen.

A young man emerged from the barn, wiping his hands on his jeans. He was probably mid-twenties, tall and broad-shouldered, with messy, windswept hair.

"Can I help you?" he asked, eyeing me and Einstein cautiously.

I gave him my best smile, trying to look mildly lost and definitely not suspicious.

"Oh! Sorry," I said. "I think I've taken a wrong turn. I was trying to get to the... Jones' place?" And I waved my hand vaguely in the direction of the hillside. There had to be a farm run by someone called Jones nearby.

The man thought for a moment, then he nodded. "You're way off for Jonesy's place," he said. "It's out the other side of Trevenna on the Polvarren road."

"I'm sorry to have bothered you," I said. I made to put the pickup into gear, then I stopped. "Are you Kyle Ingram?" I asked.

"Ye-es," he said warily.

"I only ask because Terry Grady mentioned he was doing the barn conversion for you. I was thinking of having him do a job for me. Is he a good worker?"

Kyle screwed his eyes up. "Well, Terry came out on Thursday to look at the job, but I haven't even got planning permission yet. It's still stuck in Eva Henshaw's council paperwork hell," he told me. "But Terry's a good bloke. If you've got a building job, I'd recommend him."

"Nice bluff," said Einstein, stretching on the dashboard. "Unfortunately, that gives our last suspect an alibi."

I thanked Kyle, managed to reverse out without knocking over his gatepost, and headed back toward the main road feeling miserable and defeated.

I was back to square one, with no suspects and no ideas.

Everything was hopeless.

Chapter 30

"**A**RE WE EATING AT Sylvia's again?" Einstein asked, licking his lips hopefully as I turned the pickup towards Briarvale.

I thought about my dwindling bank balance.

"No. I need to go home."

Wow. Had I just said that?

But it was true: Briarwood Gables *did* feel like home now. Unfortunately, if I didn't figure out a way to get some money coming in, I'd be negotiating with Madeleine sooner than we'd both imagined.

I was finally getting the hang of driving Tom's pickup, too, and I navigated back with Einstein only jumping in once when I threatened to make a wrong turn.

As soon as I stopped on the drive, Murphy leaped out and dashed off towards the caravan.

Was he hoping to find Tom there?

Yeah... me too.

I couldn't say I was hungry, even though I'd missed a midday meal, but felt I ought eat something, so I slapped together a sandwich and wandered into the living room. Half-heartedly, I pulled the sheets off some of the furniture, sending clouds of dust dancing in the shafts of late afternoon sunlight that shone through the window. The chairs, sofas, bookcase and coffee table were all solid wood. Polished. Beautiful.

"You had good taste," I said to my relatives, who were watching me from the faded photographs on the mantelpiece.

At least this room would only need a good clean before it could welcome guests. If I could make it that far.

Back out into the hallway, I picked up the Fifty and Freaking Out tote.

"At least I won't have much to pack," I said with a cheerless laugh.

"Huh?" Einstein jumped onto the hall table beside the bag. "Am I missing something here?"

I shrugged. "When I have to sell the house, I won't need a moving van," I explained drily. "I have a birthday tea-set that hasn't made it off the hall table, a magnifying glass I left in the library with the recipe book, an old sweater and this bag. Done."

"But you're not leaving?" he said, his whole body stiffening. "You can't leave."

"Well, unless my grandmother left some tide-you-over money, or you happen to know which book in the library hides a secret money-making spell, I'll have to."

Einstein flicked his tail impatiently. "Using magic for..."

"Yeah, yeah," I cut him off. "It's against all your magical rules. Blah, blah. I get it."

Einstein sighed dramatically. "For goodness sake, Josie. Stop feeling sorry for yourself or I'll have to insist you sleep in the library again."

"Hey, I've had a rough week," I pointed out. "You could cut me some slack."

Einstein puffed his fur out like a Persian peacock and looked me straight in the eye.

"OK," he said. "Listen up. I don't give pep talks very often, but as your magical mentor, I decree that you must embrace your newfound powers, solve the murder, and find your happily ever after in this quaint village."

I let out a laugh. "Is that your best attempt."

"Nah, I was just messing with you," he said with a chuckle. "But you know, for a witch you're remarkably unobservant. I know for a fact that you're not done with Briarwood Gables yet, Josie Appleton. Take a look at the clock."

I glanced over at it. The hands had been stuck at 3.23 for days. However, now they pointed to 11.30.

"It's moved," I commented. "But if you think I'm going to touch it again, you are one deluded cat."

"Yikes! No!" Einstein yowled in alarm. "Absolutely not. Do *not* touch it. I was hoping you'd figured out what it was doing?"

I rolled my eyes. "Well, it isn't telling the time, and honestly, I'm getting tired of riddles, Einstein. In case you haven't noticed, I'm preparing to leave, not solving the workings of temperamental magical artefacts."

I waited for him to explain, to give me a clue, but he just stared at me with his big amber eyes.

"You're not going to tell me, are you?" I sighed.

"Sorry," said Einstein. And to be fair, he did look a little bit sheepish.

"OK, am I a witch who can control time?" I asked.

That might be rather fun.

"No," said Einstein.

"But there was all that commotion about the town clock working again when I arrived," I told him. "Did it stop when my grandmother died, to miraculously start again as soon as I set foot on the station platform?"

Einstein give me an approving nod. "Now you're on the right track."

"Really? So, how does it work?"

"Magic."

I could see I wasn't going to get any more information out of him, and in the silence that followed, I heard Murphy whining at the kitchen door.

"Poor Murphy," I sighed. "This is all a big mess, isn't it?"

"And you should feed the animals," Einstein reminded me. "Tom didn't have time this morning."

I set off towards Tom's caravan with a feeling of fear and resignation.

"If Nosy Phyllis and Nosy Steve could see me now, they'd have a field day," I muttered.

Until I'd arrived at Briarwood Gables, the closest I'd come to a farm animal was driving past with the windows up to avoid the smell.

"I hope you're going to at least tell me what to do here," I said to Einstein, who was padding along beside me. "Even if you're being cagey about the clock."

Einstein twitched his tail. "Basic animal care isn't exactly advanced witchcraft," he told me.

"Not helpful."

"I know where the food is," he ventured.

"That's better."

Tom hadn't let the ducks out before he left, and Bonnie and Clyde quacked indignantly as I approached the pen. I unlatched the gate and they waddled off towards the river with the speed of London commuters running for the 8.15 train.

"Well, that was easy," I said.

"The chicken feed's in the red bin behind the shed," Einstein instructed, hopping onto a fence post like chief supervisor.

I found the bin, scattered the feed, and collected a surprisingly warm clutch of eggs without being pecked or pooped on.

Small victories.

Next came the sheep and the goat.

I crept to the pen where I'd seen Tom shut them in on the first night. Houdini was nowhere to be seen.

Presumably, he'd already found his own way out.

Mr Tuppyhead was pawing the ground, staring at me with his slitty eyes. I opened the gate and hid behind it. Just in case.

But the goat shook himself, and stomped towards the trees without giving me a second glance.

I let out a sigh of relief.

My last job was Murphy. I found Tom's stash of dog food and filled his bowl, then I waited while he gulped it down.

Job done.

My boots crunching softly on the path as I made my way back to the house. The remains of the blue and white police tape still fluttered round the greenhouse, a tattered reminder of the terrible events that had happened there. It was the one place I hadn't dared to go since the murder.

I walked along the path between the rows of early vegetables. The flagstone the police had lifted still lay on the grass, next to a dark, gaping hole.

So much for PC Waverley's promise to put things straight when they left.

I crouched down and peered inside. It was deeper than I'd expected.

Had the police dug it that far? And what had they found there? More importantly, who had buried it?

My mind drifted, unwillingly, to Tom. He was in the garden all the time. He was the obvious choice.

I shook the idea off.

"Graham called Tom with that fake job," I told Einstein. "He'd wanted to be sure Tom was out of the way. So maybe Graham came here to bury something under my path? Or dig something up? If I hadn't been zapped by the clock, I might have caught him in the act."

Einstein had nothing to add, which was rare, so I stepped round the hole and pushed open the greenhouse door.

A few early flies buzzed at the windows, trying to find a way out. There was a selection of dusty pots, tiny green seedlings, and the musty scent of damp earth.

Nothing sinister at all.

As I turned to leave, my gaze landed on the table beside the door. There, clear as day on its dusty surface, was a handprint with a police marker beside it.

I bent closer. There were no fingerprints that I could see, but the size made me stop. It wasn't large. I hovered my palm over it. This wasn't a man's print. It wasn't Tom's, and I hadn't noticed that Graham Prescott had freakishly small hands.

Had someone steadied themselves on the table when they'd bent to pick up the candlestick doorstop?

I hadn't had time to think about this before the greenhouse dissolved around me.

Now I was seeing through someone else's eyes. I could feel the weight of the candlestick in their hand. Graham Prescott was kneeling on the path. He was sneering, then his expression changed, and I watched in horror as the candlestick swung down. Graham Prescott collapsed in a heap, and a gloved hand dropped the candlestick beside him.

Then the vision swung round. There was a flash of movement outside the glass. Todd's shocked face peered through the glass.

As quickly as it began, the vision vanished, leaving me gasping for air in the quiet greenhouse.

"Josie?" came Einstein's voice.

He was standing beside me, but it sounded like it came from miles away.

"You've gone white," he mewed, peering at me in concern.

I stumbled out of the greenhouse, my legs wobbling like overcooked spaghetti.

"You won't believe what just happened," I stuttered.

"Try me," replied Einstein. "But maybe you should sit down first?"

He was right. There was a very real possibility I could fall down. I definitely wasn't done with Briarwood Gables yet.

I flopped on the bench, looking over the vegetable patch in the evening sun, my head in my hands, trying to make sense of what I'd seen.

"I got a... vision," I told him finally. "In the greenhouse... Of the murder."

Einstein's ears perked up, his cat-like cool slipping for a moment. "Psychometry? That's not possible. Or at least, hard to believe."

"Psycho-what-now?" I croaked.

"Psychometry," he repeated, his tail twitching. "It's the ability to read the history of an object by touching it. Quite an advanced skill for a novice witch. You see, the energy imprints left on objects can..."

But the garden was starting to spin. Einstein's words blurred into a distant buzz and everything went black.

"Josie? Josie!"

Einstein's voice cut through the fog in my brain. He sat on one side of me, Murphy lounged on the other.

I blinked up at him. "Wha... what happened?"

"You blacked out for a while," Einstein replied drily. "A long while, actually. It seems the power of your psychometry was too much for you. But, tell me, did you see who killed Graham Prescott?"

Chapter 31

"IT WAS A WOMAN who hit Prescott," I told Einstein. "I don't know who she was, but Todd does. He was there. He saw everything."

I hauled myself into a sitting position.

"I need to talk to Todd. Right away."

It was dark now. Long shadows pooled across the ground, and somewhere in the big trees that owl was hooting again.

Had I really been unconscious that long? I was starting to lose whole chunks of my life to magic.

Not ideal.

I staggered back to the house on legs that were still wobbly and with a head which wasn't thinking straight. I pulled my phone out of my pocket. It was half past ten. There were also several missed calls on my phone from Kim.

Poor Kim.

But I didn't have time to call and explain things. Again.

A few mouthfuls of water and a splash to my face helped to clear my foggy brain.

"Do you know where Sally and Todd live?" I asked Einstein, rubbing my aching forehead.

He shook his head.

"Well, I guess I'll have to drive about until I find them," I said.

As I gathered the keys to Tom's pickup from the hallway table, my gaze drifted to the grandfather clock. It still said 11.30.

"Something's going to happen at 11.30, isn't it?" I said slowly. "The clock doesn't keep time: it predicts the next catastrophic event."

Einstein nodded seriously.

"What happens at 11.30?"

"I don't know."

"Oh, sugar cookies," I muttered.

"But they're not always catastrophic events," he added, hopefully. "I mean, it predicted when you were arriving."

"But then its next one must have been the murder in the greenhouse?"

Einstein winced. "Yes."

My hand tightened round the keys.

Next minute, there was a loud banging on the front door.

I jumped back.

"Oh, for the love of catnip," Einstein sighed. "What fresh hell is this?"

But Murphy was wagging his tail.

Cautiously, I opened the door. A beam of torchlight caught me in the face, and there was Sally Barnes, white-faced and wide-eyed.

"Sally?" I gasped. "What are you doing here?"

"I'm so sorry to bother you at this time of night, Josie," she blustered, looking like she was about to burst into tears at any moment. "It's Todd. He's missing again, and he's not answering his phone. I'm worried sick. But I thought maybe, after this morning when he was playing with Murphy, he might have come here?"

My stomach dropped as Todd's frightened face from my vision flashed into my mind.

"I'm sorry, I haven't seen him. Have you called the police?" I asked her, trying not to sound like I already knew something was very wrong.

Sally nodded. "They said he'll probably turn up soon, but I can't just sit around and wait. I know this is different, Josie. I can feel it."

I could feel it too.

I took a deep breath, my mind racing.

"Right," I said, squaring my shoulders. "Let's go find him."

Sally turned back towards her battered Land Rover, but I bent down to Einstein.

"Hey," I whispered. "Do we have any kind of find-a-boy spell in those books in the library?"

Einstein appeared to think. "Nothing that precise, sorry," he said. "But trust your instincts, Josie. I know you'll figure it out."

"Honestly, what's the point of keeping all those books in the library, and not one of them is useful," I sighed.

As I pulled the front door shut, I caught sight of the clock, its hands still pointing firmly to 11.30. Something was coming, but I didn't know what.

Sally hovered uncertainly by her Land Rover, which was parked haphazardly next to Tom's truck.

"Come with me in the pickup," I told her. "I'll drive and you can keep a proper look out for Todd."

I didn't add 'and you look like you shouldn't be driving', but the way her hands were shaking, I didn't think she should.

Sally hesitated only a moment, then she nodded and climbed in beside me.

Murphy jumped into the footwell, and Einstein settled himself on the dashboard.

"I let Todd have the day off school and we had a good chat this morning," Sally told me as I turned the key. "Or I thought we did."

I bit my lip. No matter how well she thought the conversation had gone, she didn't know he'd witnessed a murder?

But why hadn't Todd gone to the police? Had the killer threatened him? No wonder he was acting so off.

"He's not handling the sale of the farm well," Sally went on. "He kept saying we should have held out for more money, and that he was going to fix everything."

"Fix everything? How?" I asked.

Sally shrugged. "Then this afternoon, I had an appointment to see a new house on the Trevenna road," she said. "I thought it would give Todd something to look forward to, but he hated it. And when Madeleine started going on about being able to get us a better deal on the house, he just... walked out." Her voice cracked. "I haven't seen him since."

I stopped, my hand on the gear lever.

Madeleine!

Suddenly, everything started to click into place.

In the HoneyPot, Madeleine was wearing driving gloves, just like the ones I saw in the vision I'd had in the greenhouse. And gloves meant she'd leave no fingerprints.

Intentional or co-incidence?

I didn't know.

And there was that woman-sized handprint in the greenhouse.

I didn't know *why* she'd kill Graham Prescott, but every part of me screamed that she had.

"What time is it?" I asked, eyes on the road as we rumbled down the drive.

Sally checked her phone. "Five to eleven."

Time was running out.

Chapter 32

W E DROVE SLOWLY DOWN the lane into Briarvale. Sally's head jerked left and right, scanning every shadow that could maybe conceal Todd.

I was sure this had something to do with Madeleine. Todd had seen what happened, something she wouldn't want him talking about. He could be in serious danger. I had to figure out where they'd go.

The village was quiet. Only the sound of laughter and chatter came from The Briar and Thorn, the warm glow from the windows lighting up the street.

Sally nodded towards it. "It's Edwin's domino night," she said. "I didn't like to disturb him. And I've already called all Todd's friends. I don't know what else I can do."

We passed through the village and out the other side, where Sally spotted Doctor Hale walking up the garden path of a tiny cottage with wisteria covering its porch. It appeared Annie wasn't the only villager whom the doctor had converted to his healthy eating plan.

"I think Todd's disappearance has something to do with Madeleine," I ventured.

Sally turned sharply to look at me and frowned. "Why on earth would you say that?"

How could I explain the visions and magical clocks and weird greenhouse imprints without sounding completely bonkers?

"Just a hunch," I muttered. "Do you know where she lives?"

Sally hesitated.

Obviously, I sounded mad enough without giving her all the magical details.

Then she nodded. "The top of Briar Hill. She bought it after old Mr Trevelyn died. It needed a lot of work, but rumour has it she got it for a knock down price." She motioned behind us. "You'll have to turn round."

Madeleine's house was an impressive double-fronted place at the end of a lane. It was covered in scaffolding and surrounded by dumpy bags of sand and a cement mixer.

"She's not here," said Sally, surveying the empty drive. "Her car's gone."

That only increased my fear for Todd.

My stomach tightened. "Where are you, Madeleine?" I muttered as I made an awkward twenty-point turn among the builder's rubble.

"Umm, did Madeleine seem... normal when you saw her earlier?" I asked.

Sally thought for a moment. "Well, she was in a hurry to leave," she told me. "It was the planning meeting at the council for that scheme she has for the old mine, so she was itching to go. But then after Todd walked out, I didn't want to stay either."

I gripped the steering wheel. That was it!

"Do you know where Silverbrook Mine is?" I asked, an icy dread creeping up my spine. Something was going to happen at 11.30, and somehow, I had to stop it.

"Kind of," she said. "I've never been."

"I know the way," said Einstein, his eyes glittering in the darkness. "Emily... she was two witches before your grandmother... her husband worked there. Turn right past the station."

The headlights on the pickup cut through the darkness as we barrelled down the winding backroads.

"What time is it?" I asked Sally.

"Umm, 11.15."

I pressed my foot harder on the accelerator.

"Turn left here," called Einstein, a fraction too late.

I slammed on the brakes. The tyres screeched and we skidded across the road, sending Einstein sliding across the dashboard with a startled yowl. I threw the pickup into reverse and swung us onto an even narrower side road.

"Almost missed that," I muttered through gritted teeth.

"I think it's somewhere down here. On the right," said Sally in a shaky voice.

"Umm... Sally," I said, as calmly as I could manage. "I think you should ring the police. Tell them where we are. Tell them Todd's been kidnapped. Because I think he has."

"Kidnapped? Why would you think that?" she gasped, but she was already fumbling with her phone.

"If I'm wrong, you can blame it on me," I told her.

Sally punched 999 into her phone.

Einstein was standing on the dashboard now, peering into the darkness. "Slow down," he said. "The turning's not easy to spot. Just a narrow gate, and it's a bit different than when I used to come with Emily."

I eased off the accelerator, squinting into the darkness. There, half hidden by a huge oak tree, was a rough, dirt track. Tacked to the tree was a crooked sign which read 'Keep Out', and underneath that someone had stuck a recent planning notice.

"Yes, kidnapped. That's what I said," Sally was saying into the phone. "Todd's been kidnapped. We're on our way to Silverbrook Mine right now. You need to come."

The track was bounded on each side by wild hedges which caught the sides of the truck as we bumped along. Grass grew in the middle, but it looked flattened. Someone had definitely driven along here recently.

"The police are on their way," said Sally.

"Good. What time is it now?"

"11.22."

Eight minutes. Whatever was going to happen, we didn't have much time.

The track widened out into a small clearing, which reminded me of the set of one of those low-budget horror films that Gary had liked to watch. Crumbling buildings. Overgrown weeds. And a mineshaft blocked by rotting old timbers. The kind of place where some axe-wielding maniac would appear at regular intervals and make everyone jump.

"There!" Sally shrieked suddenly, pointing at a neat hatchback pulled between two rickety buildings. "That's Madeleine's car."

I stopped the pickup at the end of the lane. If Madeleine made a run for it, she wouldn't get her car past the pickup. I turned off the engine, but I left the headlights on, flooding the yard with a hazy yellow glow.

Sally reached for the door, but I caught her arm.

"Wait," I said. I set my phone to video and propped it on the dashboard next to Einstein. "If this goes wrong, someone needs to know what happened."

Sally nodded.

"Stay," I told Murphy, as we stepped out into the glare of the headlights.

The gravel crunched impossibly loudly under our feet as we walked towards the mine entrance.

"Todd," I called, my voice echoing eerily off the rusty corrugated walls.

Nothing.

"Todd!" Sally yelled.

The wind rustled the trees overhead.

Still nothing.

I took a deep breath. "Madeleine!" I shouted, praying I sounded braver than I felt. "I know it was you who killed Graham Prescott. But Todd's a kid. You don't want to go there."

Just when I was beginning to think we were too late, a figure appeared in a doorway.

"Todd!" Sally choked as he came running towards us at top speed.

He flung his arms around her. "I'm sorry. I didn't mean..."

"It's OK," said Sally, holding him tight.

I think they were both crying.

"Let's get you home," she said.

But another figure had appeared out of the shadows.

Madeleine.

In her hand was a gun.

"Don't anybody move!" Madeleine shouted. "Because I *will* shoot."

A gun was definitely not part of my non-existent plan.

"Madeleine, please," I said, trying to keep my voice calm. "You don't have to do this."

"You don't know what I have to do," she snapped, but I could see her hand trembling slightly on the gun. "You think you're clever. You think you've figured it all out? Fine. You want answers? Let me give you some."

Madeleine paced back and forth, angrily muttering to herself, her ankles twisting in her usual high heels. "This should have been easy," she muttered. "Undervalue the Barnes' farm - get a cut of the profit. But that lying, cheating Prescott got more than he told me. Far more. Buried the money under the flagstones at Briarwood Gables. Thought I wouldn't find out. But I did."

"What? Todd was right: you cheated me out of my farm?" gasped Sally.

"And Briarwood Gables was to be Graham's next project, but then *you* turned up," she said, waving the gun at me accusingly. "He told me you weren't an easy sell, like he'd hoped, so he decided he had to move the money. He was really surprised to see me, but he laughed! Said I should be grateful I'd got anything at all. And there was the candlestick by the door. I didn't mean to kill him. I just wanted what was mine."

"But Todd saw, didn't he?" I said quietly.

Madeleine's mouth twisted. "And *he* wanted money too," she groaned. "He said he wouldn't tell anyone if I paid him. The cheek of it! But I thought if I lured him to the mine and waved the gun about it would scare him off. Then he ran, and you showed up, and now..." Her hand trembled. "Now everything's ruined."

"Hey, look," I started. "No-one's going to say anything about this. We can all leave and..."

"Shut up," Madeleine cut me off, swinging the gun wildly.

I moved to shield Sally and Todd. The gun pointed straight at me.

"Why did you have to start poking around?" she growled. "Now I have no choice."

"No, we can talk this through," I stuttered.

In the distance, the Briarvale clock chimed the half hour.

"No. No more talking," shouted Madeleine.

An ear-splitting shot shattered the night.

Sally screamed.

Todd screamed.

I think I screamed too, instinctively throwing up my hands: a hopeless defence against a bullet. And in slow-motion, I watched it streak through the air towards me.

Chapter 33

S OMETHING WAS HAPPENING.

There was a crackle of electricity. A flash of light.

An energy I didn't know I had surged through me and burst from my hands. The air shimmered, and the bullet veered off into the bushes as though swatted by an invisible hand.

Madeleine was thrown backwards, like she'd been hit by a hurricane. The gun flew from her hand and clattered to the ground.

And just like that, it was over.

Madeleine lay motionless in the dirt, out cold. The gun skittered across the path, out of reach.

I stood there, hands still raised, a faint tingle of magic fizzing at my fingertips.

Sally and Todd stared at me.

"W... what happened?" Sally stammered.

"I... I think Mrs Appleton stopped it," Todd choked. "She stopped the bullet."

"No," I stuttered. "No... umm... Madeleine stumbled on those silly shoes she wears as she was taking the shot. Looks like she knocked herself out as she fell."

The wail of approaching sirens cut through the silence.

With a jolt I realised that magic had just saved my life. My magic. This wasn't a silly family quirk. It was real.

I was doing my best not to pass out... again. Somehow, I made it back to the truck. Murphy jumped out, running excited circles around everyone, herding his humans.

"Well," said Einstein, as I collapsed on the seat. "That was interesting."

It was a long night.

There were explanations. Then statements. Then more explanations.

Flashlights. Notepads. The sound of radios crackling.

I showed them the video on my phone. It hadn't caught everything, but it caught enough. Madeleine's confession. The moment she raised the gun. Then there was the flash of magic, the way the bullet veered off course.

Officers huddled around the tiny screen. Rewound it. Played it again.

"That's a lens flare from the headlights," one officer suggested. "Happens when there's a sudden motion and a strong light source."

"Could be a reflection off the gun barrel," said another. "The gun looks nickel-plated. Those things catch the light like you wouldn't believe."

"Or interference on the phone camera," said a third. "Cheap lenses don't always handle sudden contrast well."

"And Madeleine definitely flinched," said one of the officers. "Pulled the trigger too hard. It happens, even with experienced shooters."

And I nodded and agreed with their theories. So long as they didn't yell 'that was magic and she's a witch,' I didn't care.

DI Holloway arrived halfway through, stone-faced and tired-looking. He listened and asked a few clipped questions, scowling at me like I was a problem he didn't have time to solve right now.

"You were lucky, Mrs Appleton," he said. "But you put yourself in danger. In future, leave the police to handle these situations." Then he stalked off to bark orders at someone else.

Madeleine was taken away in an ambulance, still unconscious. The gun was bagged as evidence.

Eventually, someone handed me a blanket. Someone else said I could go.

Todd and Sally hugged me tight. Murphy tried to climb onto my knee, tail wagging furiously, while Einstein looked at me with what might just have been newfound respect.

The sky was beginning to pale at the edges when we finally pulled away.

I didn't say much as I drove home. I don't think I had anything left to say.

It was ten o'clock when I woke up the next morning. I wouldn't have woken then, but someone was knocking on the door.

Groggy and still wrapped in the tail end of dreams about guns and uncontrollable magic, I padded to the front door in my socks. Murphy bounded in front of me, his tail already wagging like he knew exactly who was on the other side.

The moment I opened the door, Murphy launched forward with a joyful bark.

Tom barely had time to brace himself before he was body-slammed by twenty-five kilos of ecstatic sheepdog. Murphy whined, wiggled, and licked Toms face with wild abandon.

"OK. OK, Murph. I missed you too," Tom laughed. He dropped to his knees. "Alright, alright, you're going to knock me over."

PC Waverley stood behind him, grinning. "I don't know which of them has been looking forward to this reunion the most, but I thought I'd give Tom a lift home. It was the least we could do." He turned to go, then he stopped. "Oh, and DI Holloway says, and I quote, 'tell Mrs Appleton not to even think about starting a detective agency'. Though between you and me, I think he was almost impressed with the way you solved the case."

After he'd gone, Tom stood up, his face flushed from too many dog kisses. We stood there looking at each other, uncertain what to say.

"I drove your pickup," I blurted. "I hope you didn't mind."

"Mind?" said Tom. "I've heard all about how you solved the case and cleared me. You can drive the truck any day."

"And you can use the shower," I told him.

"Well, I might take you up on that," said Tom. "But first, I'm going to see to the animals. Thanks, Josie."

I spent the morning finally investigating my house, pulling dust sheets off forgotten furniture, peering into mysterious cupboards, and poking in drawers full of long-lost knick-knacks.

Starting in the hallway, I cleaned the floor, knocked down the cobwebs, and dusted every surface, but I was sitting cross-legged on one particularly sumptuous four-poster bed, looking in an old biscuit tin full of buttons and foreign coins, when my phone buzzed with a video call.

Kim.

"Hi, love," I said, smiling cheerfully.

"Mum! Oh, thank heavens," Kim burst out. "I was beginning to think I'd have to jump on a plane and come and rescue you."

"Don't be silly," I chided gently. "I've been a little... busy. I'm very sorry I missed your call."

"You've missed *many* calls, Mum," Kim corrected. "I've not spoken to you since Saturday."

"Ah, well, let me see," I said. "Sunday I was at the Briarvale Great Runaway Egg Festival. There was a band, some line dancing... and I may have fallen down a hill chasing a runaway egg. But don't worry," I added quickly, seeing her face. "There was nothing broken."

"Right," said Kim, clearly not convinced. "And yesterday?"

"Ah, yesterday." I hesitated. "A rather dreadful estate agent kidnapped a friend's son and then tried to shoot me. But she had terrible aim, and the bullet ended up in a bush."

There was silence.

Then Kim laughed. "Mum! Be serious."

"I am being serious."

Kim's eyes narrowed, "OK. Where's Dad? He's not answering his phone. And don't give me rubbish about a bad signal."

I took a deep breath. "Well... he *might* have a bad signal," I admitted, taking the easiest question first. "I don't imagine the reception is great... in Paraguay."

Another pause.

"Why is Dad in Paraguay?" asked Kim slowly.

"His business has gone bust," I explained gently. "It happened on my birthday. We've lost the house and the car, and he's gone." Once I'd started, the truth poured out. "But I'm fine. I'm staying at Briarwood Gables, and it's lovely. Well... except for the man murdered in the garden on my first afternoon. And the rather stern detective who mistakenly arrested Tom. Oh, Tom's the handyman who lives out back. But it's OK now. I got him released."

I stopped, watching Kim's face alternate between horror and total disbelief.

For once, Kim had nothing to say.

There was a pounding on the front door.

"Look, love, I have to go," I told her, scrambling off the bed. "Don't worry about me. I'm having a ball."

And it was true.

I just hoped that whoever was at the door wasn't carrying a gun.

I raced down the stairs.

The knock came again, followed by a yip.

Eva and Florence, complete with Charlie, who was sniffing something interesting in the wisteria, stood on my porch.

"We've come to collect you," Eva announced. "There's a celebration at the HoneyPot for Tom, and the murder being solved. And thank heavens, that ridiculous spa proposal is officially dead." She beamed as though she had defeated it in single combat.

Florence nodded. "We thought you should be there, because it's all thanks to you, really. You're the woman of the hour."

"Or the witch of the hour," remarked Einstein, appearing at the door with the swagger of a heavyweight champion. "You've got more magic than anyone thought. I can see you're going to be great fun."

I didn't know whether to be pleased about that or not.

Charlie growled when he spotted Einstein.

Einstein blinked slowly. He drew himself up to his full height, which was easily twice the size of Eva's dog, and fluffed up his fur.

"Boo," he hissed.

With a frightened yip, Charlie retreated behind Eva's legs. I tried not to laugh.

"Charlie still doesn't like cats," Eva muttered, though she might not have sounded quite as judgemental as before.

"Einstein doesn't like dogs," I said, laughing as he stalked off, victorious.

Eva stepped inside, and I was suddenly glad that I'd cleaned the hall. "Hmm. Someone's been busy," she said grudgingly. Her eyes landed on the tea-set, still on the table. "Oh my, that's Wedgwood," she said reverently, tripping over to inspect the box. "Bone china. Lovely pattern."

"Would you like it?" I asked on impulse. "It's more your style than mine. I'd be terrified of chipping it."

Eva was momentarily speechless, which I took as a personal achievement. "Well... I mean... I couldn't possibly..."

"Yes, you can," I said firmly. "Consider it a thank-you to the welcome committee."

Eva clutched the tea-set to her chest like it was her firstborn child.

Not wanting Florence to feel left out, I grabbed the Fifty and Freaking Out tote bag. "You liked this, didn't you?"

Florence's eyes lit up. "Oh! Oh yes! It's very... bold."

"Just like you," I said, handing it over in a cloud of flying glitter.

And with that, we all piled into Eva's car, Einstein on my knee, and set off for the HoneyPot.

There weren't enough seats for the number of villagers crowded into the tiny tearoom. Sylvia was down to using her emergency crockery, which meant I got a chipped mug with a picture of a dancing bumblebee on the side.

It was perfect.

I squeezed on a table next to Sally and her children. Sally gave me a hug and even Todd managed a brief nod.

"I can't thank you enough for last night," said Sally. "But I don't know what I'm going to do. The farm sale's off! The buyer's being investigated for fraud. Something about fake invoices and offshore accounts. Madeleine and Prescott weren't the only snakes in the grass."

"Why don't you keep it?" I said.

She looked at me, startled. "But I can't manage it on my own."

"Maybe you don't have to." I looked round the room. "You just need to ask for help."

There was a murmur of approval from the gathered crowd.

"And what if you teamed up with Terry Grady?" I went on, in a flash of inspiration. "His building firm's struggling after that job Prescott cancelled, but he's already got materials sitting around and you've got barns going to waste. You could turn them into holiday lets. Profit share."

The table went quiet for a beat, then Sally blinked. "That's... actually brilliant."

"Profit share," repeated Terry thoughtfully. "It could work."

"You're following right in the Stanton problem-solving tradition," mewed Einstein, cleaning his whiskers after finishing the cream Sylvia had provided. "Your grandmother would be very proud."

The bell over the cafe door jingled and Tom walked in.

Everyone clapped. Someone cheered. PC Waverley gave him a thumbs up. And Sylvia appeared carrying a slightly crooked cake with 'Welcome Home' on it.

Tom hastily sat down across the table from me, looking like a man who'd rather be fixing a roof than being congratulated for not being a murderer.

"We knew it wasn't you," piped up Poppy. "Silly Detective Hollowbrain got it wrong."

And everyone laughed.

Sylvia handed me a piece of cake and I sat back in my chair, letting the chatter and laughter wash over me.

For a moment, I wondered what Gary was doing. Was he sitting in a coffee shop in Paraguay? Did they have coffee shops in Paraguay? I realised I really didn't care.

There was so much still to sort out to turn Briarwood Gables into a B&B: licences, linen, registering with the council, but maybe Eva would help with that now she had her Wedgwood.

And then there was magic to learn. My father was wrong. Crazy Beatrix hadn't been crazy at all.

Or maybe I was becoming Crazy Josie?

I took a bite of cake. It was so much better than my birthday at Crème de la Crumb. Briarvale was as kind as it was nosy.

And it wasn't like a murder would happen again in sleepy Briarvale, would it?

·✦ · ✹ · ✦ · ✹ · ★ ·

Josie and Einstein have solved the murder. But when the judge at Briarvale's annual folk dancing festival drops dead, they're back to causing chaos on the case with their magical baking in *Signed, Sealed and Deadly.*

·✦ · ✹ · ✦ · ✹ · ★ ·

If you loved Josie and Einstein's story, you can help other readers solve the crimes in Briarvale by *leaving a review*. Just a couple of lines saying what you liked about the book will be great.

·✦·★·◆·★·★·

Curious how murder and magic first tangled in Briarvale? Join Josie as she dives into her grandmother Beatrix's diary and uncovers the truth. Download the free prequel, *Destiny, Diaries and Death* and uncover the secrets that started it all.

WITCHY @ 50

BELLA COLBY
books

Printed in Dunstable, United Kingdom